I0518907

TOMORROW

Book Five of the Yesterday Series

A Novel By

Amanda Tru

Published by

Sign of the Whale Books™

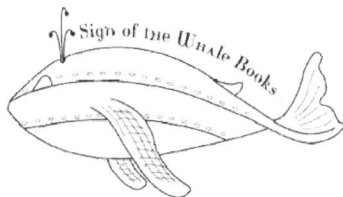

PUBLISHED BY: *Sign of the Whale Books*™*, an imprint of *Olivia Kimbrell Press*™, P.O. Box 4393, Winchester, KY 40392-4393. The *Sign of the Whale Books*™ colophon and Icthus/spaceship/whale logo are trademarks of *Olivia Kimbrell Press*™.
**Sign of the Whale Books*™ *is an imprint specializing in Biblical and/or Christian fiction primarily with fantasy, magical, speculative fiction, futuristic, science fiction, and/or other supernatural themes.*

Original Copyright © 2014.

Cover Art and Graphics by Debi Warford (www.debiwarford.com)

Library Cataloging Data
Tru, Amanda (Amanda Tru) 1978-
 Tomorrow, book 5 in the Yesterday Series/Amanda Tru
  233 p. 20.32cm x 12.7cm (8in x 5in.)

Summary: Trapped in the wrong tomorrow, can Hannah find her way back to yesterday?

     ISBN: 978-1-939603-81-4

1. time travel 2. christian romantic mystery 3. new adult 4. male and female relationships 5. paradoxes

[PS3568.AW475 M439 2012]
248.8'43 — dc211

TOMORROW

Book Five of the Yesterday Series

A Novel By

Amanda Tru

TABLE OF CONTENTS

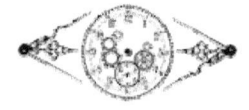

CHAPTER ONE

I had traveled back in time and saved my sister's life.

And the cost?

My husband's life was now spilling out all over me and the pavement beneath us.

"Help!" I yelled, my voice thin and gasping. "Seth has been shot! Call 911 and get Wayne!"

I didn't look to see if my mom or Abby were following my instructions. Instead, I focused on Seth. I held his head in my lap as I pushed the sleeve of my coat on the wound bleeding from his chest.

"No, God! No!" I moaned, praying frantically yet with little coherence. This couldn't be happening.

Seth's body was shaking. His breathing was becoming erratic.

"Hang on, Seth." I murmured, stroking his face with the fingers of my free hand. "Hang on. Wayne's on his way."

Seth's eyes looked up at me, the moonlight reflecting the color of a tropical sea. "… love… you…"

"No, Seth, no!" I panicked. Sobs constricted my throat, and I couldn't breathe. "Don't leave me!

"… backpack…"

Seth's backpack! It had everything in it. Maybe it had something that could help.

I gently set Seth's head down and scooted out. As I stood, a familiar headache came crashing down. I had returned to my original time, and now my body faced the consequences. I felt darkness closing in, threatening to steal away my consciousness. I fought it off, stumbling to where Seth had left his backpack a few feet away.

I lifted the pack and unzipped it. I reached inside, though I didn't know what I was looking for.

I turned back to Seth.

The Golden Gate Bridge rose in the background; it's beautiful, romantic lines now a giant, hulking shadow. The soft moonlight bathed Seth's body, lying still on the deserted pier. The soft glow caught his eyes as they stared up at the stars, unseeing.

He was dead.

"Nooooo!" I screamed, the chilling, agonizing sound echoing through the trees and across the bay.

I heard my mother's voice as she ran to me, trying to soothe and comfort, trying to keep me calm even from a distance.

But my gaze remained fixed on Seth. His chest would never again rise in breath; his beautiful eyes would never see.

Then, as uncontrollable grief irresistibly beckoned, the pain in my head suddenly fled, and I watched as Seth's dead body dissolved before my eyes.

My mother's voice faded. It felt as if I was sinking into warm, deep water.

Then I surfaced. My surroundings came back into focus. And my headache was gone.

I was still on the pier. The bay was still to my back. The Golden Gate was still at my side.

But my husband's body was gone.

As my bone-chilling scream echoed across the bay, my hands covered my eyes as if trying to block the image seared there. But it didn't help. I could still see Seth's eyes in my mind. They were the same blue-green that had captured my heart from the beginning, only they were devoid of life and staring straight up.

I had time traveled, but that didn't change the reality of what had just happened. Though I could no longer see his body, Seth was dead. It didn't matter whether I was in the future or the past. This day and every day after would be a day without him.

I ran.

Without conscious thought, my legs propelled me down the dock. My sneakers hit the pavement of the road, and still I ran.

All of my instincts screamed for me to escape. If I could just run fast enough and far enough, then the events of this place might dissolve into nothingness. It would be like a book. If I could just close the book on this setting, then I could escape to a new one and believe that the past few minutes hadn't existed.

I wanted to put as much distance as possible between myself and the dock. I didn't even notice the road or think about which direction to go. I ran in a straight line, heading directly up a hill into thick brush. Trees reached their branches out to grab me. Bushes and vines tangled under my legs to trip me. The heavy silence muffled my sobs.

The moonlight flitted above the trees as I staggered uphill. I stumbled repeatedly, picking myself up each time and charging on. I didn't know or care where I was going, as long as it was away.

"Oomph…"

I ran head-on into something. The full-length of my body plastered against something solid, knocking out my air and stopping me as if I'd run into a brick wall.

As I fell back, I saw it was a fence. It's tall and compact structure left no way to get through.

Without hesitation, I turned to the left and ran again, angling back through the trees as I tried to run along the side of the hill.

Two minutes later, I came out of the brush and plowed once again into another section of fence.

Confused and disoriented, I stepped back. The second impact had penetrated my emotional haze, causing a small amount of rational thought to slip into my mind.

Though my feet longed to turn once again and run, I was lucid enough to pause. The tall, straight structure extended through the darkness as far as I could see. It looked almost like a security fence, not allowing any holes that even a worm could penetrate. It felt strange that I didn't remember seeing a high fence surrounding the area when Seth and I had arrived in the taxi.

Still feeling the overwhelming urge to escape, I turned back to the right and ran alongside the fence.

I knew the high structure had to end somewhere, but the stress of being trapped only added to my desperation to escape.

My breath came in increasingly shorter gasps. My lungs burned. Yet I still kept running. Every time numb relief would crowd close, the image of Seth's body would flash through my mind. A scream of agony would lodge in my throat, and my feet would propel me to flee with renewed energy.

It wasn't real... It wasn't real. My mind whispered the same mantra over and over again to the rhythm of my pounding feet.

I followed the fence back down the hill. As my feet left the vegetation to connect with pavement, I found where the fence finally ended in a gate spanning across the entrance to Fort Baker Pier.

I couldn't see how the gate was latched. There didn't seem to be a chain or a lock. My hands shook as I reached out to the cool metal, hoping to push or pull it out of the way.

A loud, ear-piercing alarm sliced through the air. I jumped back from the gate, my body practically convulsing with shock and fear. Though my hands no longer contacted the gate, the alarm continued its shriek.

I spun around, almost expecting to be spotlighted by a helicopter and blinded by the flashing lights of law enforcement. Though darkness was still my only companion, I knew that would change in a matter of moments. The alarm would gain the attention it demanded. But when the authorities arrived, how would I explain being found inside a locked area? They would ask how I had managed to get onto the pier without setting off the alarm. Obviously, the system would have been designed to keep people out, not in. It would be the equivalent of being found inside the locked vault of a bank. There was no way to believably explain my presence.

All of this flashed through my brain in a matter of seconds and panic gripped me. I needed to get out of here. Looking back up the hill the way I'd come, I knew I'd find no escape in that direction. I turned to my right and followed the line of the fence in the opposite direction, past the gate to where it met the water down by the dock.

Hopelessness washed over me, and I knew there would be no way out. What was the use of a fence if it didn't fully enclose something? No matter which direction I chose, it wasn't going to eventually stop and provide a convenient exit.

I heard sirens in the distance. Maybe I could hide! I took a few steps back toward the trees and brush, but just as quickly, I stopped. People who bothered to equip this area with a security system of this kind weren't going to leave without a thorough inspection.

If they knew the alarm had been tripped from the inside, they would also know that I hadn't been able to leave. Hiding anywhere in the fenced area would just assure that I would eventually be found. They might even shoot first and ask questions later.

I trembled. The sirens were getting closer. At any second, police vehicles were going to round the corner and catch sight of me standing in the beams of their headlights.

I was trapped.

Desperately, I spun and ran down the pavement, back to the pier. I didn't have a plan, but I knew I needed to be as far away as possible from those who would be coming after me. My feet hit the long dock, and without pausing, I ran down the full length, only to finish exactly where I'd started. Nearing the end of the pier, I picked up Seth's backpack from where I had left it. I clung to it, longing for the comfort of a familiar object.

As I slung the backpack to my back, I turned to face the spot where Seth had died. I studied it, transfixed, as if I expected his body to reappear at any moment. But I was the one who had left, not him. On this day in some time, Seth's body still lay lifeless.

The flashing lights of the police cars broke the spell and drew my attention up. Brightly lit vehicles were pulling up to the end of the dock.

They were coming for me.

I backed up until I felt a metal railing against the spine of my mid-back. I was at the very end of the pier and could go no further. My gaze flitted over the water. There was nowhere left for me.

Dear God!

It wasn't a prayer. Everything that was happening was my fault. I hadn't wanted God involved in my life or my decision to save my sister. He was the one who had taken her away to begin with.

But it was a cry of despair.

I saw the figures of officers appear at the end of the dock. As a shout reached my ears, fear and desperation took over.

I climbed up the railing, and, without thought or an instant of hesitation, I jumped into the black waters of the bay.

CHAPTER TWO

THE instant I hit the water, my brain caught up and I realized I'd just committed suicide. It was December. There was no way I could survive the temperature of the bay without a wetsuit.

As if on autopilot, my body began to swim. I had always been a good swimmer. I might have become a lifeguard as a teen, except I didn't think the skin of a redhead could handle the constant burning and freckling of a summer spent poolside.

Now the cold was my enemy, though the water didn't feel as freezing as I expected. I wondered if that was just a delusion caused by the numbness of hypothermia, but I reassured myself with the knowledge that the temperature was still cold enough to take my breath away and demand that my body move to escape certain death. As my arms pumped and my legs kicked automatically, I realized what my body was doing.

As I'd run toward the pier, I had noticed that, while

the fence had ended at the water's edge, a wire barrier had extended into the bay following the dock. But it hadn't extended all the way to the end of the pier. It didn't need to. Boats would need to have access to the dock. Besides, the fencing was to prevent people from visiting the area after hours. Nobody in their right mind would have the desire or need to swim around the barrier to get to the outside.

Maybe my unconscious mind had realized that the only escape would be to get around the fence. Now, as my sense caught up, I plotted my course across the inlet to the right of the dock. With brief glimpses in between strokes, the moon offered enough light to see the shadow of the shore and some lights straight across the small bay.

Seth's backpack pulled at my back, weighing me down and making swimming difficult, but I wasn't willing to let it go. I tried to swim at an angle that would let me pass the wire barrier, yet get me to the shore the fastest.

But the darkness and water in my eyes made seeing increasingly difficult. Every once in a while, I caught sight of my blurry destination, but it felt mostly like I was swimming blindfolded.

Adrenaline propelled me forward. Numbness took over, replacing the feel of the cold water and heavy backpack. Faced with the fight or flight instinct, my body had chosen to flee with a determination that trumped all fear, rational thought, and even the fact that I couldn't see where I was fleeing to.

I don't know how long I swam. It felt as if I'd been swimming forever, yet then I was at the shore, pulling my body out of the bay and hurrying to join the shadows. I could hear shouting. I waited breathlessly for the space of several seconds, focusing on the direction of the voices. Had someone seen me jump in the bay?

With the echo from the water and the distance, I couldn't understand the shouting, but at least it didn't seem to be getting closer. Maybe I wouldn't be followed.

My entire body was shivering uncontrollably. I didn't know what hypothermia felt like, but I knew I felt colder than in my entire life. There was a slight breeze coming from the direction of the ocean that only served to worsen the profound chill on my body. My only chance was to get out of the wet clothes. My trembling fingers struggled to unzip Seth's backpack. I knew everything in there was going to be soaked, but I was desperate.

As I yanked at the zipper, I could hear loud music reverberating from a building to my left. I glanced up to see boats lining a dock that extended into the small bay I'd just swum across. Though I couldn't inspect the boats or see any posted signs, my immediate guess was that it was a yacht club.

I was finally able to open the backpack enough to slip my hand inside. The interior of the backpack was sopping wet, but feeling something plastic, I pulled it out the hole. It was a large freezer bag with a zippered seal. By the light of the moon, I could see that it contained cash—a lot of cash. I thrust my hand back into the bag and pulled out several more large, sealed bags. One of them had a shirt folded neatly inside. The other one had a pair of sweat pants. I didn't know how or why Seth had thought to pack things in waterproof containers; at that moment, I didn't care. I'd always known that Seth was a meticulous planner whose organization could border on obsessive-compulsive at times, but if I hadn't been so unbelievably cold, I would have wept tears of relief.

I quickly pulled off my shirt, my pants, and even my soaked undergarments. Just as quickly, I replaced them with the dry shirt and sweat pants. I wadded up my wet clothes and stuck them in the backpack along with the bag of money. Though drier, I was still cold. I knew I still needed to find somewhere to dry my hair and warm up, but I was better.

Holding the wet backpack away from my body, I turned and climbed up the slight, rocky embankment from the water's edge.

"Nice swimsuit," a voice said.

Startled, I looked up to find a man standing only a few feet away. He'd obviously been close enough to have a full view of my quick wardrobe change. I felt his gaze as he completed a thorough inspection from my wet hair to my shoes that squished with every step.

Clearing his throat, he spoke again. "I didn't realize that kind of swimming was popular in this part of California, but if you let me know your schedule, I'm sure I can arrange to put on similar attire, or maybe I should say *take off* my attire."

I would have normally blushed crimson at the thought that this man had seen me naked, but I was already so emotionally traumatized that I just didn't care. He sounded young, and although I couldn't see his features clearly, I would've guessed him to be in his late teens or early twenties. Realistically, he was probably a college student out partying at his wealthy parents' yacht club.

"Is there a hotel nearby?" I asked, completely ignoring his comments and obvious assumption that I had been skinny dipping.

"Sure," he answered. "Right up there on the hill."

He would have said more, but I cut him off. "Thank you," I said, marching past him and heading in the direction he'd pointed.

"Do you want me to show you the way?" the young man offered eagerly.

I didn't answer, hoping that my lack of response would do more to discourage him than any words I could voice. I didn't look back, but trudged up the hill with purpose. Hopefully the hotel wouldn't be too hard to locate.

I was out of breath, but not any warmer as I neared the top of the hill. It wasn't exactly a gentle slope, but the cool night breeze kept my teeth chattering despite the physical exertion. Stopping to catch my breath, I looked up. As my eyes made contact with bright lights lining a building at the crest of the hill, my stomach dropped. I knew I had found the hotel, but it wasn't just a hotel; it was a resort.

Knowing that I didn't have a choice, I strode with determination to the front door and tried to muster up as much dignity as I could. As I inched forward in the rotating front door, I held my wet head high and tried to ignore the fact that I was wearing my husband's old sweats. My shoes squished and squeaked slightly across the glossy, tiled foyer as I marched directly to the front desk.

"I need a room," I confidently told the front desk clerk who'd been watching my grand entrance with a slightly gaping mouth.

He cleared his throat. "Do you have a reservation?" he asked politely.

"No, I don't," I answered, trying to keep the trembling from affecting my voice. "But I'll be paying with cash."

"I'm sorry, ma'am, I think you have the wrong hotel. It is 1:30 at night. There is a pay by the hour hotel somewhere in town, I believe." The scorn in the man's eyes was obvious, and it clearly had chased away his manners.

I knew how I must look, but I had reached my limit. The man looked so self-righteous. His bald head was tipped back so far the overhead lights reflected off his forehead as he looked down through a small pair of glasses perched on his long nose.

"Do you not accept cash?" I gritted out.

"It is our prerogative to refuse guests for any reason," he shot back haughtily. "I believe you would be happier at one of the other hotels. May I call you a cab?" He reached up and straightened his little bow tie. It was a superior gesture that called attention to the stark contrast of his expertly ironed, expensive suit and my wet, bedraggled appearance.

"Are you telling me that you have no rooms?" I asked

sarcastically. "I am a paying customer, offering to take one of your vacant rooms in the middle of the night. I somehow doubt you have other customers arriving tonight. Are you really willing to refuse the payment for a room that you would otherwise get no money for tonight?"

"I don't believe you have the resources necessary to pay for the room," the man replied, as if he was looking down the nose at some pesky ants who dared disturb him. "No one pays for a hotel room in cash. In all my years working here, it hasn't happened once. Perhaps a little too much partying tonight has made you over-estimate your funds. At $430 a night for one of our rooms, I really think you would be more at home in another hotel."

The man actually thought I was under the influence of something!

Wordlessly, I opened Seth's backpack and began rummaging around for the bag of cash.

Clearly impatient to get rid of me, the clerk leaned over the counter, trying to get my attention. "If I can't call you a cab, ma'am, then perhaps the police would better suit your needs." He picked up a phone and pushed a button.

"Henry, are you seriously such an arrogant snob?"

I recognized the voice and whirled to find the young man from the shore, stepping up to the counter beside me.

He gave me a concerned yet slightly chastising look. "I told you to just mention my name."

Turning back to the clerk, he glared and spoke again.

"But you wouldn't think name dropping would be so necessary for a paying customer. It's amazing to think that, in this day and age, people are still so unfairly judged on their appearance."

The man named Henry looked startled and turned a little green, as if he'd been sucking on something sour. "You know this woman?"

"Of course! I'm the one who told her to come up here after she fell in the water down at the yacht club! I wanted to pay for her room; I was the one who accidentally knocked her in. But she refused my offer, saying that she could pay for her own room. She didn't want people making assumptions if I was the one to pay, but I guess people don't need an excuse to make stupid assumptions."

The man's hands fluttered around like the feathers of a flustered chicken. "My apologies, Mr. Richardson. I had no idea. Of course we will be honored to accommodate a friend of yours in one of our rooms."

"At the member discount rate, I hope," the young man said with expectant, raised eyebrows.

"Of course," Henry assured, eagerly bobbing his head. "That will be $250, Miss. Now if you'll just sign our register here, I will get your room keys."

Henry handed me an electronic tablet, similar to an iPad. I quickly skimmed through the standard legalese, including the policies and rules associated with the hotel. I hurriedly checked boxes, marking my breakfast preferences. Then I positioned the stylus to sign at the bottom.

I knew better than to sign my own name. I paused as my mind flitted through about a dozen possible aliases. Unable to cover the slight ironic quirk to my mouth, I confidently signed the name *Katherine Colson* and counted out a wad of money from my stash.

Henry handed me the key card, and I quickly strode to the elevator with the young man, Mr. Richardson, in my wake. My room was on the second floor, but I wasn't sure I'd make it if I tried to use the stairs. The stress of the past few minutes had combined with my freezing body to make my muscles feel like rubber bands stretched so tight they may snap at any instant.

I pushed the button, and the elevator doors immediately slid open. I paused, my eyes sidling to my rescuer beside me. He was young, just like I'd thought. I would have guessed his age to be about 21. He had neatly-trimmed, light brown hair and had an easy, boyish smile that lit up his hazel eyes. As my eyes met his, he winked conspiratorially, and I could tell he was struggling to hold in the laughter over his scamming of Henry.

Thank you! I mouthed silently. Then I hurried into the elevator and pushed the button for the second floor. I had no idea why Mr. Richardson had helped me get a room, but as the elevator doors slid shut on his smiling face, my rubber band muscles snapped with the sudden relief, leaving me so weak that I almost melted to the floor with the elevator's upward motion.

The doors slid back open on the second floor, and I hurriedly found my room. My hands were shaking so bad that it took me three tries before I was able to slide the card into the lock on the door. At the sound of a happy beep of success, I pushed open the door, closing it quickly behind me. I slid the dead bolts, and then turned and ran for the bathroom, pulling off my clothes as I went. I turned the shower on and slid the knob as far to the left as possible. I stood violently shivering, waiting until the water hitting my outstretched hand became warm.

Finally, I got in. Increasingly hot water cascaded over the goose bumps covering my entire body, though it took about ten minutes of standing in the shower before I finally stopped shaking. The water was scalding, hot enough to turn my flesh pink, but I made myself turn the temperature down only slightly. There was nothing to compare to how wonderful the water felt after being so very cold.

But as my body temperature warmed up, the dam of tears thawed. With the immediate danger now passed, I started to feel. I took deep breaths and closed my eyes, trying to stop tonight's events from replaying through my head. But it was the emotion I couldn't escape. Sobs strangled all breath from my throat, yet it was a silent cry. It felt like a nightmare where I was trying to scream yet couldn't make a sound.

Seth was gone! He was dead, and it was my fault!

I reached up and held the locket around my bare neck, as if it was a lifeline to the world as it should be. I rarely ever took it off, especially after Abby had died. To me, it had become a sort of emblem for the possibility of changing history. After all, the locket had belonged to my biological mother in the future when I'd been born. If time travel had saved me, why couldn't it save Abby?

But now, that hope was gone. Time travel hadn't brought me the one thing I'd wanted. Instead, it had taken away the one person I couldn't live without.

My entire body filled with overwhelming agony. I wilted, curling into a fetal position as I lay at the bottom of the tub. I longed to cry, to release some of my emotion, but the hot spray cascading over me only symbolized the tears I could not shed.

I had felt grief before, overwhelming, uncontrollable grief. But this was different. It was a spiritual grief as well. Because of my actions, my entire world was now devastated. Up until this point in my life, I had leaned on my faith. I couldn't do that now. Those who mattered most to me were now gone. I had gotten Seth killed, and I had walked away from God. Without my husband and my faith, I was completely and utterly alone.

In one part of my mind, I expected to time travel again. I had never felt such intense anguish. I would likely end up completely naked and in the shower in a different time, though at that moment, that wasn't a detail I really cared about.

But there was one idea that did bother me: the thought that I may travel back to the time I'd just left.

Sudden fear pulsated through me so strongly that I dragged myself up off the bottom of the tub and turned the water off. I grabbed a soft, fluffy white towel. As I dried myself off, I fought for control. My shoulders still heaved in great, silent sobs, but I couldn't face the risk that I may travel back to where Seth's body lay on the dock awaiting a funeral and burial. It was cowardly and probably wasn't even a real risk, but that did nothing to ease my sudden fear.

Though Seth and Wayne had warned me that I could travel multiple times in close succession, tonight had been the first time it had ever happened. The theory was that extreme emotion produced a spike in a chemical in my brain. This chemical, tempamine, is what triggered my time travel. Supposedly, if the tempamine spiked and I traveled, there was a possibility that it could spike again in rapid succession, producing another jump through time.

However, multiple jumps due to extreme emotion had never happened. Even tonight, I had relaxed to return Seth and I to our correct time, but then the trauma of Seth's death had likely triggered another spike.

Could I travel again if the grief became overwhelming?

Until now, extreme emotion had only caused me to make a single leap, and the only way I had ever gotten back to my own time was by relaxing, which supposedly caused a decrease in the tempamine levels. But the logic of my experience couldn't stop the fear. In my mind, whenever I was now, it was preferable to an unknown alternative, especially one that could potentially involve Seth's dead body.

A white robe with an embroidered hotel logo hung invitingly by the door to the bathroom. I slipped into it and went over to the sink, though I avoided looking in the mirror. If I saw the grief and stress marring my own face, then I was afraid it would breathe fresh life to the thoughts and feelings I was trying to push down.

Between Seth's healthy stash of supplies in the backpack and the complimentary toiletries, I was able to brush my hair and my teeth. I kept my mind blank, focusing on the lights and the sound of the toothbrush swishing against my teeth. As I finished and walked into the main room, the sight of the bed caused me to stop with a sharp, painful intake of breath.

The light of the bedside lamp released a soft glow over the room. I was sure that this wasn't the most elaborate room the resorted boasted. In fact, it really resembled more of a standard hotel room in terms of size and features, though the décor looked richer in its quality and colors of gold and wine.

It was the sight of the sateen bedspread as it lay turned down that made me choke on sudden sobs.

I would be sleeping alone tonight.

A mere twenty-four hours earlier I had been lying beside my husband, cuddled in the bed of a cabin at Silver Springs. I felt his warmth as he'd held me, speaking words of comfort. He had said it would all be alright. He had said he had prayed.

Seth had been wrong.

Either Seth had misheard God, God hadn't heard Seth's prayers, or God just didn't care. Either way, everything was not okay. And it would never be okay ever again.

My thin veil of control slipped away as a rogue wave of grief hit me full force. The emotions were breathtaking in their intensity. Confusion, anger, sorrow, and longing all vied for priority. I was angry at God for letting this happen, angry at Seth for lying about it all being okay, and angry at him for the greater crime of dying.

As white hot fury gave way to sorrow, I felt ill. Not being able to stand any longer, I lay across the bed. I grabbed a pillow and crushed it to my chest as if I was trying to hold onto Seth himself.

This was only the first night of forever. Seth would never again lie beside me. I would never again feel his arms holding me close or taste his kiss on my lips.

I had inadvertently made a trade. I had tried to save my sister's life, yet I'd sacrificed my husband's in the process.

I clutched the pillow to my chest until it restricted my breath. I squeezed my eyes shut, blocking out the lonely hotel room in a foreign time, the memories of the past twenty-four hours, and the sound of my own sobs. I shut everything out and tried to bury myself in a dark box where nothing could reach me. Maybe if I stayed in the box long enough, I could wake beside my husband to find that it had all been a dream.

CHAPTER THREE

I felt the pressure of Seth's body at my back. As the threads of sleep gradually lost their hold, I stretched my muscles and smiled. Waking up beside my husband was one of my favorite things in the world.

My mind filled with memories of last night and his gentle caresses and passionate kisses.

In one smooth motion, I rolled and propped myself up, thinking to wake Seth with enough kisses to trigger his memories of last night as well. I parted my eyes just a slit, but the bed beside me was empty.

My eyes flew wide as instant panic took hold and the real memories of yesterday vibrated though me like high voltage. What my dream-numbed mind had thought was Seth pressed against my back, was actually just a pillow.

I picked up the offensive object and threw it at the wall as hard as I could.

Heart pounding, I jumped off the bed. The entire

stock of memories had come back in one instant, but arriving with the past from yesterday was a new determination. Whereas paralyzing shock and grief had been the predominant emotions last night, anger immediately took over this morning. I knew what I had to do. I needed to go back and fix it. I needed to save Seth.

A nagging voice in my head accused that trying to change history was what had created this tragedy in the first place, but I quickly gagged that suggestion. There was no way I was going to let my husband die, not if I had the power to save him.

I had deliberately changed history before; after all, I had saved Abby. I could do it again. There was no decision to make. Without Seth, there would be nothing left for me. I would save Seth even if it cost my own life.

I glanced at the digital alarm clock on the nightstand. My heart gave a mighty leap into my throat. It was 11:30. I was supposed to check out of my room no later than noon!

I ran to the door, unlocked it, and peered into the hall. A tray sat waiting in the same place as it had probably been for the past few hours. I picked it up and scurried back to the safety behind my locked door. Thankfully, the tray had been equipped with an impressive, little warming pad, so my food had stayed fresh. I grabbed the TV remote, sat on the bed, and quickly dug into the eggs, bacon, and gooey cinnamon roll. The food was good. At least, I think it was. I ate it so fast that the only opinion I was absolutely certain about was that the cinnamon roll, though delicious, wasn't as good as Abby's.

Trying to multi-task, I turned on the TV. I really

wanted to find a news program that might tell me the date or give me some information about when I was.

The screen lit up, but it was unlike any TV I had ever seen. Curious, I slipped off the bed and padded closer. The screen was very thin and flat. I saw there were several gadgets in the cabinet below the computer / TV, but I didn't bother trying to figure them out. Instead, I reached out my finger and gently touched the surface. A little arrow appeared. It was a touch-sensitive computer. While some aspects of the screen seemed familiar, it looked like it was running a version of Windows 1,000!

In the right hand corner of the screen was the date. As I stared at the year, I tried to swallow the lump in my throat.

Ten years. I was ten years in the future.

Thankfully, the computer's operating system seemed to be a future version of one current to my time. I was able to quickly access the internet. I found good-ole' Google and typed in 'Dr. Wayne Hawkins.' Numerous sites popped up on the screen. I scrolled through them quickly, not clicking on any of them. I was looking for something specific. I didn't have time to catch up on Wayne's life or read about any of the research, awards, or accomplishments from the past ten years. I just needed an address.

Not finding anything that looked promising, I scrolled back to the top of the page and clicked on the first link, hoping that it might contain the most recent information.

Pictures of cars zoomed across the screen as a big banner unfolded across the top. A car dealership? Why would Wayne's name be associated with a car dealership? Then I saw his picture under the heading 'Sales Representatives.' It was an older, balding version of Wayne, but it was still him.

A sick feeling twisted in my stomach. If Wayne was working at Marin Autoplex as a used car salesman, then I already knew this future was a bizarro world version of what should be. In the correct timeline, Wayne was a gifted medical research doctor. Something catastrophic must have happened to change that.

With a sharp intake of breath, I remembered that this wasn't the first time I had encountered Wayne as a used car salesman. Before I had time travelled and changed history for Wayne, I remembered Seth saying that his best friend had been kicked out of medical school and had become a used car salesman. But I had changed all that. I had prevented Wayne from taking the blame for Katherine Colson's drug habit. He hadn't been kicked out of school, but had instead become a brilliant and successful doctor.

A wave of despair enveloped me as a soft voice seemed to whisper that maybe this was how it was supposed to be. Maybe Wayne was meant to be a car salesman, and I had interfered with providence.

I shut my eyes and shook my head. "No," I whispered. Then I repeated, louder and more firmly, "No!"

Everything in me rebelled against the idea that this was the way things were supposed to be. Wayne should be a doctor, not a used car salesman. And Seth should not be dead! There was nothing right about this future.

I really had no choice. I had to change it.

The thought flitted through my head that maybe I shouldn't be the one to fix it. Trying to fix it myself is what created this mess. But I quickly dismissed the idea. With Seth's life on the line, I was up against the same dilemma I'd had with Abby. I couldn't trust anyone, especially God, to fix history the way I knew it needed to be.

I'd screwed things up; I would be the one to fix them.

Seeing a notepad lying on the nightstand, I grabbed it and the matching hotel logoed pen and hurriedly jotted down the address of the car dealership. Clicking the little location insert map, I recognized a few of the street names from Sausalito and tried to pinpoint in my mind exactly where Marin Autoplex was located.

Though I was desperate for a few more minutes to research more what had happened in the past ten years for Wayne, a quick glance down to the right-hand corner of the screen showed that I was out of time. Wayne would just have to tell me himself once I found him.

After sticking the notepad and pen in Seth's backpack, I quickly shrugged into Seth's clothes that I had worn last night. My other clothes were still wet, so I shoved them back in Seth's backpack along with all of my other belongings and the hotel logoed envelopes and samples of shampoo, soap, and whatever else disposable I could find. My natural tendency was to always prepare for the worst. Since I was pretty sure my current circumstances qualified as 'the worst,' I had no qualms about taking even the little package of coffee, though I hate the stuff. One never knew what uses one might find for bad coffee when traveling through a distorted future.

After running a brush through my hair and cleaning my teeth, I shot one last, longing glance at the shower. How I would love to climb back in that sanctuary one last time! Knowing I only had about five minutes before the clock struck noon, I resolutely zipped up the backpack, hefted it to my shoulder, and left the room.

If I was going to change history, I couldn't spare any more time or energy on grief. I had to find Wayne. Car salesman or not, he would still be the same genius and one of my few forever friends. He would know how to help me fix everything.

I hurried to the elevator and down to the lobby. Though the new clerk at the front desk eyed me a little suspiciously, I checked out without a problem. I turned and headed to the front doors.

"Hi! I figured you'd be checking out around noon. Did you sleep well?"

I stopped short as the tall, lanky Mr. Richardson from last night reappeared alongside me.

CHAPTER FOUR

I looked at the young man in surprise. Had he been waiting for me?

But my slightly creeped-out feeling fizzled in the light of his boyish grin and innocent, unassuming manner.

"I slept fine, thank you," I replied in a monotone. I turned and continued toward the door, hoping that he would get the hint.

I marched down the steps with Mr. Richardson still following in my wake. When I got to the sidewalk, however, I paused, uncertain of which direction to take.

"Can I give you a ride somewhere," the young man asked eagerly.

A flat refusal died on my lips as I paused, seriously considering his offer. I had no way to get to the car dealership. I had looked at the map on the computer enough to know the general vicinity of my destination, but I hadn't had time to really study how to get there from here or figure out exactly how far of a walk it would be.

"I just need to go to the downtown Sausalito area," I said stiffly.

"Sure!" Mr. Richardson said enthusiastically. "I'll be happy to give you a ride. Follow me. My car is over here in the parking lot."

A small little voice from my youth warned me that you should never get in a car with a stranger. But I had already lost everything of value to me, and though I wanted to set things right, beneath my determination was a large part of me still hemorrhaging grief to such a degree that I had little regard for my own safety.

I followed him to a shiny red convertible sports car. It said Malibu on the side, but the design looked different from the sports cars of ten years ago. Mr. Richardson held the car door open for me and then went around to the driver's side.

I spent the first few minutes of the drive in turmoil. The convertible top was down, allowing the air to whisk past and lift my hair in gentle waves. He drove slowly, not nearly fast enough to erase my anxieties.

I wished he hadn't opened the door for me. It was a sweet gesture, but one that made me think he might have gotten the wrong impression when I accepted his offer of a ride. On the other hand, I was in sweats and looked terrible! There was no way he's interested in more than friendship. At least, that's what I told myself.

"I'm Bryce, by the way," Mr. Richardson said,

cocking a flirtatious eyebrow my direction.

"And I'm married," I blurted out, holding out my occupied ring finger as evidence.

"Happily?" Bryce asked, not missing a beat.

"Yes!" I shot back, shocked. "Very happily married!"

Bryce shrugged, completely unfazed. "It doesn't really matter. I'll still give you my number just in case. Life happens. Maybe you won't be so happy tomorrow. Maybe your husband will be a jerk. Maybe you'll just need a little... entertainment. My number is very easy to call."

My mouth literally fell open at his brazen audacity. I stared at him as if he was a strange, previously-undiscovered species. The planes of his boyish face were relaxed, the front of his brown hair stood up in cocky little spikes, and an annoyingly confident half-grin lifted the corner of his mouth. I was so shocked that I couldn't formulate an immediate response.

Bryce threw his head back and laughed at the look on my face. "Don't look so surprised!" Returning his gaze to the road, he continued in a more serious tone. "Your name is Katherine, right? I saw you write it when you registered last night.

As his eyes flashed my direction, I gave a slow, hesitant nod as my dazed mind tried to respond. *Katherine, my name was Katherine.*

"Don't you feel it, Katherine? Don't you feel the connection we have? I feel like I've met you before, like your beautiful image is something I instinctively recognize. I've never been one for poetry or mystical stuff, but I somehow feel like I know you. Maybe in some cosmic way, we belong together."

I forced myself not to roll my eyes. Bryce was sincere, and I really didn't want to hurt him. I had no idea what connection he was feeling, but it wasn't reciprocated by me. It seemed ridiculous that this obviously wealthy young man could be attracted to the scraggly, no make-up version of me in sweats. But then again, I guess he did see me naked, though I honestly didn't think that could account for the man having lost all reason!

Staring ahead at the road, Bryce continued with confidence, as if determined to vindicate his noble motives. "This connection is not something I encounter every day, so you'll have to excuse me being bold. If I see something I want, I go for it, no matter what stands in my way."

I didn't want to crush him. But I needed to be clear. "Bryce, you flatter me way too much, but I am madly in love with my husband. Nothing is going to change that—not the cosmos… or even death." I took a deep, shaky breath. "I appreciate everything you've done for me, but we can only ever be friends."

"Maybe. Maybe not," Bryce said with a shrug. "I think I'll take my chances."

This time I did roll my eyes as I turned to look out the window. There was no use trying to reason with him. I could see clearly that he was going to cling to his delusions, no matter what I said. The only option now was to ignore him and come up with a highly-effective subject change.

"There are a lot more trees and flowers than I remember," I mused, looking out at the passing foliage. The hills surrounding the resort were covered in green while the roadway was lined with flowers. The entire area appeared as if it had been professionally landscaped.

"You can blame that on the Natural Regeneration Act," Bryce offered, thankfully responding to my pitiful attempt at a subject change. "I know the act succeeded in putting a lot of Americans back to work in replenishing the vegetation in urban areas; I'm just not sure they achieved the 'natural' part."

I nodded as if familiar with the policy responsible for the garden around me. "I certainly don't remember the Bay Area as being so tropical," I agreed, eying a display of small palm trees and huge, red, lily-like flowers.

Bryce laughed. "I think they must have purchased plants in bulk for the entire state of California. They probably even have palm trees on top of Mount Shasta!"

"Can you drop me off here at the corner?" I asked, suddenly realizing we were only a few blocks away from the car dealership.

"Are you sure?" Bryce asked hesitantly.

"Yes," I assured. "I'll be meeting a friend."

Bryce reluctantly pulled over to the curb.

After the experience with the taxi driver last night, I didn't want to let Bryce know my exact destination or give him any information about me. After being chased through the streets of San Francisco, our taxi had taken us to where we were to meet Seth's contact and hand over the evidence about the effects and massive cover-up of a harmful anti-depressant medication. But Katherine Colson and her conspirators from Jones-Stanton Pharmaceuticals bribed the taxi driver into telling them where he'd taken us.

They had found us and brought with them my worst nightmare. I had managed to time travel and get us away from capture and further gunfire, but not before Seth had been shot. The moment I'd seen Seth's lifeless eyes staring up at the sky, I had once again been swept through time to ten years in the future; ten years from where I had been last night.

If the taxi driver hadn't given away our location, or if Seth and I had thought to have him drop us off away from our actual destination, then maybe we would have never been found and Seth would still be alive. I wasn't going to take the risk of trusting anyone with my whereabouts until I knew exactly who and what I was up against.

"I'll give you my number," Bryce said as I opened the door to get out. "Put it in your phone and give me a call if you need anything."

"I don't have a phone," I answered flatly. At his questioning look, I shrugged. "It got a little wet last night."

Amusement lit Bryce's eyes at the mention of my apparent skinny dipping. I hadn't even bothered to look for my phone. It had been in the pocket of my jacket. If it was still there in my jumble of wet things, then it would be thoroughly ruined. Not that it mattered. It wasn't as if my cell phone plan from ten years ago would still be active and the phone functional.

Bryce reached down in the center console and lifted out a card. He leaned across the seat, offering it to me with outstretched hand and an attempt at a beguiling expression. "Here's an old-fashioned business card. I thought my dad was nuts when he insisted I get them, but I guess they are useful."

I knew it would be easier to just take the card rather than to waste the time and energy trying to refuse. "Thank you," I said politely, then quickly turned and walked down the sidewalk. I turned the corner and waited until I saw Bryce's car pass the intersection. Then I turned around and went the opposite direction.

With the street names from the map in my head, I was able to walk a few blocks and find the dealership easily enough. Though it was a used car lot, every 'used' car I saw probably cost more than most people made in a year. They were all luxury vehicles of some kind, and some of the models were ones I had never seen before.

I wanted to be subtle in approaching Wayne. I didn't want to approach him in a group where we might be confronted with questions that would be difficult to find explanations for.

So I snuck around the lot like a thief, alternately peering over the hoods of cars to identify figures standing in the next aisle, and then ducking around so as not to be seen. There were several salesmen with customers scattered around the lot, but I didn't recognize any of them as Wayne. Unfortunately, I was afraid the only way to find Wayne would be to go directly to the showroom and ask for him.

Giving up in my reconnaissance of the car lot, I scurried toward the large showroom doors. In the first aisle directly in front of the door, I saw him. He looked so different, especially from a distance. But I knew it was him, almost as one can recognize their own facial features. Despite the balding hair, extra fifty pounds, and tacky suit, I knew Wayne Hawkins.

He was speaking with one of his coworkers. I patiently waited while they finished their conversation, but the intermittent guffaws were aggravating when I was crouching behind a sports car waiting to get some help with a pretty significant crisis!

The other salesman finally walked away, and I stepped out.

"Wayne," I called softly.

At my voice, Wayne swung around to face me, his eyes wide and wild. Before I knew what was happening, Wayne rushed at me, quickly pushing me behind a large Hummer.

"Who knows you're here?" he demanded in a fierce whisper

Shocked at his reception, I fumbled for words. "N-No one knows."

"Hannah, you have to tell me!" His wild eyes flashed around as if afraid the vehicles were watching and listening. "Where have you been for the last six months?"

"What are you talking about?" I asked, thoroughly confused. "Six months? I haven't been here for six months. I landed here last night after I watched Seth get shot and die. Apparently my yesterday was ten years ago, not six months!"

I took a deep breath and struggled to calm myself to answer Wayne's questions in a way that would satisfy him. "I stayed overnight at a hotel, and then I came directly to find you. No one else knows I'm here, aside from the kid who gave me a ride into town, but he doesn't even know my name."

Wayne stared at me, and I saw his throat constrict as he swallowed. "That's impossible," he whispered.

"What are you talking about?" I asked, mystified. Wayne's dramatic manner and cryptic whispers were becoming frustrating.

"Hannah, what was the date yesterday, the day you and Seth were at the pier and Seth got shot?"

"December 19th," I said matter-of-factly. "Abby was killed on December 19th. That was the day I wanted to change, and apparently I did. But then Seth…" I shook my head and took a deep breath. "But that was yesterday. Today is December 20th, but it's apparently ten years later."

"Ten years and six months," Wayne corrected quietly.

"What?" I asked as a chill raced down my spine.

"That's why I thought you had been here for six months. Hannah. You always travel in yearly increments. But today is not December, Hannah. It's June."

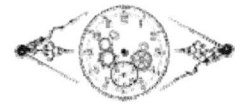

CHAPTER FIVE

BEFORE I could utter a gasp, Wayne took hold of my arm and propelled me to fall into step beside him.

"Come on," he gritted, his eyes dashing to and fro as he weaved a circuitous route between the vehicles. "We can't talk here."

Even though I hurried to match Wayne's frenzied pace, Wayne still kept a grip on my arm, pulling me along with him. He led me around the exterior of the showroom to a back door. Using a key, he unlocked it and pushed me inside ahead of him.

We went down a narrow hall until Wayne urged me into a room labeled with his name plate. After shutting the door securely, he turned to me.

"We still can't talk here," Wayne said hurriedly. "It's too dangerous. *I'm* too dangerous. You shouldn't have come here."

"Where else would I go Wayne?" I said, traces of

hysteria threading my voice. "I need help! You're the only one who can help me."

"I can't help you. They're watching me! Always. For the past ten years. I think they knew you'd eventually show up and come looking for me. Now you have."

Chills raced up and down my body, and my throat constricted. I wanted to know what had happened to create such fear in one of the bravest, most intelligent men I knew. What repercussions had my actions caused in the past ten years? I needed to know. But Wayne didn't give me the chance to even ask.

"Meet me down at the ferry in an hour," he ordered. "We'll talk on the trip across the bay. I have a job over there tonight as it is. But after that, you leave and never contact me again. Understood?"

Wayne didn't wait for my response. He went to his desk, opened the large, bottom drawer, and pulled out a box. He then returned to the door. As quietly as possible, he opened it a crack and glanced nervously down the hall. "I figured you'd land somewhere on the timeline and find me. I just figured it would be December, not June. There are things in the box you can use for a disguise so hopefully you won't be recognized. I've gathered them over the years. And now it has arrived—the day I've been dreading. I didn't expect it to be now though. I always thought you'd show up in December."

Wayne was obviously flustered. His hands moved to and fro nervously, and I noticed a twitch in his eye. It didn't seem as if he was thrown so much by my presence as by my timing. I had no idea why this time was different. Why hadn't I traveled in yearly increments like every other time? Wayne was apparently disturbed by the same question. If I had shown up December 20th, the same day I'd disappeared, maybe he'd have been better in control. Having me show up in June was probably a possibility that had never occurred to him. Now, my unexpected appearance had already threatened Wayne's plans as well as a tenuous grip on his composure.

Wayne led the way across the hall and deposited me in the restroom. With his hand on the knob to shut the door, he turned to look at me. Stress created a maze of lines in his forehead. "After you're done, take the white Ford Spirit out the back door and meet me at the ferry station in exactly one hour. The keys are in the car."

I wanted to ask what exactly a 'Ford Spirit' was, but not wanting to risk any questions to further complicate the tangled lines on his brow, I thought I'd take my chances and figure it out on my own.

"Do what you need to make yourself unrecognizable, Hannah," Wayne's voice came as a quiet hiss as the door began to shut. "And for goodness sake, do something about that hair!"

I locked the door behind Wayne. Then I turned to the mirror. I looked haggard. The only color on my pale face was the dark circles beneath my eyes. Wayne was right. I had to do something about my hair. It waved like a red flag, announcing my grand entrance to a time I didn't belong.

I opened Wayne's box to find it stuffed full with an assortment of scarves, hats, makeup, hair dye, and other accessories. I picked up a bottle of black hair dye, opened it, and looked in the mirror.

I positioned the bottle next to my hair and tried to imagine myself with the pitch-black hair it advertised. Though I preferred to dub my long hair to be 'auburn,' most people ignorantly called it 'red.' Sometimes it appeared more toned-down than outright red; at least, I liked to think so. I had often wondered what it would be like to dye my hair. However, if I happened to voice the thought aloud, friends and family would object, maintaining that my natural hair color was beautiful. Now was my chance. It was too dangerous to keep the red.

Yet, why was I hesitating?

I reached up and thoughtfully wrapped a lock around my finger. Seth loved my hair. I remembered the feel of his fingers tangling in the long strands as he kissed me. I remembered how he sometimes liked to brush my hair while we watched a movie together.

The image in the mirror blurred as I tried to see through unshed tears.

I couldn't do it.

I had nothing left of my husband. I was going to do everything I could to go back in time and save him. But there was no guarantee that I would succeed. At this moment in time, he was dead. And he had been dead for the last ten and a half years. I may not be able to change that. With grief so overwhelming, I may never be able to travel back in time to even try, let alone relax enough to get back to my correct time. I may be stuck here, and Wayne seemed to think that would be a very bad, dangerous thing.

If I dyed my hair, even though it would be the logical, safer thing to do, it would be like erasing a connection to Seth. Getting rid of my red hair would be equivalent in my mind to getting rid of the ring finger of my left hand. Danger or not, I just couldn't do it.

I returned the hair dye to the box and instead took out several scarves. Using a loose hair band from the box, I knotted my hair up on the top of my head and then wrapped bright, colorful scarves around it. The end result was that, with every strand of hair carefully concealed, I looked like a cancer patient.

Deciding that I might not blend in well with such a look, I pulled out a hat from the box and mounted it atop the scarves. The hat was a light blue and brown combination that was almost like a slouchy beanie. It masked most of the square footage covered by the scarves, and I thought made me a little less obvious.

Turning to the makeup, I quickly slathered on whatever would make me look worse, not better. I made the circles under my eyes even darker and drew on a few delicate wrinkles. I finally added a pair of glasses. At the bottom of the box, a long, beige trench coat was neatly folded. I shrugged it on and packed everything else back in the box.

With one last, approving look in the mirror, I confirmed that I looked completely ridiculous. Hopefully that was just ridiculous enough to pass through the streets of the San Francisco Bay Area without attracting attention.

I carefully twisted the doorknob and peeked out the bathroom door. Seeing that the coast was clear, I hurried across the hall and slipped back into Wayne's office. I walked over to his desk and replaced the box in the bottom drawer where I'd seen Wayne remove it.

At the sight of Wayne's computer, I hesitated. Wayne had said I needed to meet him in an hour. That meant I had plenty of time. How was I going to manage to waste another forty-five minutes anyway? It would only take me about fifteen minutes to get to the ferry terminal.

Deciding quickly, I turned on the computer and sat in Wayne's chair. I had to find answers, and Wayne was acting so strangely, this might be the only chance I would get.

Wayne's computer wasn't nearly as high-tech as the one at the hotel had been. It still had a touch screen, but its operating system wasn't as new. It more closely resembled what I was used to from my own time.

I glanced uneasily at the door. There was no way to lock it. The showroom building sounded silent with not an echo of a footstep. But if someone did come through the door, I would have nowhere to hide and no defense.

As the Google homepage appeared on the screen, I typed in two very familiar words, 'Hannah McAllister.' The results were instant. Major news websites appeared at the top of the list—CNN, NBC, ABC--with headlines leaping off the screen. My hand clamped over my mouth to stifle the scream that would surely escape.

"Hannah McAllister—A True Black Widow"

Dateline NBC—"Web of Deceit: The Hannah

McAllister Story"

"Hannah McAllister Named in Top 5 of America's Most Wanted"

Wikipedia was the fourth on the list. I clicked on it and brought up a long page complete with some of my childhood and high school graduation pictures. Frantically, I skimmed the entire page, each paragraph increasing the sickening feeling of horror. When I reached the end, I went back up to the beginning and started again, reading more carefully and trying to make sense out of something that was worse than any nightmare.

There was very little truth behind the Wikipedia article, but that didn't matter. The events that were spelled out were the reality for this distorted future, and there was no escaping the fact that I had been thoroughly and completely framed for a host of heinous crimes.

Ten years and six months ago, Hannah McAllister, a brilliant chemist, murdered her husband, Dr. Seth McAllister, by shooting him to death at Fort Baker Pier. Her motive was thought to have been twofold. It was rumored that Dr. McAllister was having an affair with an unidentified woman, and it was also believed that he'd discovered his wife's secret. She killed him out of anger over his affair and to keep him quiet about the fact that she was solely responsible for the distribution of a commonly used anti-depressant that had led to harmful side effects and death, affecting potentially thousands of patients. Hannah McAllister was labeled a mass murder and perhaps even more villainized because she completely and mysteriously disappeared after murdering her husband. It was thought that she may have escaped by boat to South America.

There were more awful details, but I skimmed over them until I found a list of Hannah McAllister's known associates. Wayne Hawkins name was highlighted in blue, indicating it as a link to another Wikipedia article. I suspended my mouse over it and clicked. Wayne's biography popped up. I scrolled down to the bottom, finding the most recent updates to his life story.

A door slammed. I jumped, my hand jerking off the mouse. I held my breath, waiting for the sound of footsteps on tiled floor. Staring at the doorknob, my eyes strained to detect any twist of movement. Nothing happened. No one came, but no one left either. There was no sound announcing the exit of whoever had entered the building.

I glanced down at the time perched in the right, bottom corner of the screen. I needed to get out of here. I couldn't be late to meet Wayne. Besides, the longer I waited, the more chance there was that I would be found by whoever might be wandering the building.

The little arrow of my mouse hovered over the button that would shut the computer down. I hesitated. Wayne was right. He wasn't safe for me to be around. He would be considered one of my known associates. It sounded as if my fictional story had reached urban legend status. It was an unsolved mystery on the scale of the famous hijacker, D. B. Cooper. They would come after me. I didn't even know who 'they' might be for sure, but it sounded as if those searching for me likely included all of America!

How could I have a hope of not being apprehended and arrested?

An idea suddenly hit me. I exited out of the Wikipedia article and went to the browser history. I quickly deleted the trail of the sites I had visited in the past few minutes. I didn't have the time to go through for a more thorough deletion of the browser history, but having the sites absent, at least superficially, should slow down whoever might be looking to track me.

I spent the next few minutes leaving a trail of bread crumbs. I didn't know if they would look for me here. I didn't know if they would search Wayne's computer. But if they did, I wanted to send them on a wild goose chase.

I heard a door slam again. And then voices echoed through the building.

I shouldn't be here! Wayne would assume I'd left long ago. My trembling finger finally clicked the button to shut down the computer. As I stood and turned to the door, I glanced back at the computer as the thought flitted through my head that maybe I should try to wipe my fingerprints off everything.

But the drone of voices continued, and I knew I couldn't risk the time it would take to erase the evidence of my presence. As comforting as it may be, if they were searching Wayne's computer, they probably already knew I'd been here. It wouldn't matter if my fingerprints confirmed it or not.

I carefully twisted the doorknob and pulled slowly, trying to open the door as soundlessly as possible. I could hear the voices clearly now. They sounded as if they were coming from the showroom at the front of the building. Holding my breath, I snuck my head around the edge of the door.

With a quick glance both directions to confirm that the coast was clear, I soundlessly shut Wayne's office and sprinted on my tiptoes to the back door. As I pushed the heavy door open, it screeched in protest, the sound reverberating down the hall. I abandoned all attempts for subtlety and ran, letting the door fall shut behind me with a bang.

A small gray car sat waiting in the left-most parking space. I didn't waste time searching for a logo, but since it was the only vehicle in the area, I assumed it was the Ford Spirit Wayne had instructed me about. At my insistent tug, the drivers-side door opened, and I jumped inside.

At any second, I expected to once again hear the bang of the door as the owners of the voices came out to investigate. I snatched up the key fob laying on the center console, but there was no actual key attached to it. It looked like a standard black key fob, except that one end looked like it could be plugged into the USB port on a computer.

But how was I supposed to start the car with no key? I frantically pushed every single button inlaid in the plastic.

The engine suddenly roared to life. I looked down at my finger firmly squeezing the third button, which must be an automatic ignition. I put the car in reverse, and my foot found the gas pedal. As I shifted it back into drive, I hit the gas hard. I cringed as the tires squealed their excitement, but I didn't look back to see if anyone noticed my grand exit from the parking lot.

With the map from the internet still fresh in my mind, I didn't have trouble navigating my way to the Golden Gate Ferry Terminal. I did, however, take precautions by traveling a circuitous route to get there. I checked the rearview mirror frequently, and although I didn't think I was being followed, I didn't want to take any chances.

As I drove, I took in the streets of Sausalito and felt like an idiot. How could I not have realized it wasn't December? Flowers in all shades bloomed everywhere from the center divides in the roadway to climbing trellises on buildings. Everything looked like an elaborately-maintained garden where a weed dared not lift its head.

However, despite the beauty, I could see that Bryce had been right. There was a definite tropical feel to everything. Though the landscaping was done very artistically, I couldn't get used to seeing hordes of palm trees and tropical lilies.

In my defense, I did have some good excuses for my earlier lack of observation.

Though the Bay Area didn't have Southern California winters, flowers did grow year round, but not the same type or profusion as down south.

Besides the landscape, I'd had enough trauma in the past two days to interfere with my thought processes for at least a couple of decades.

Added to that was the distraction of Bryce.

But probably the greatest reason for completely missing the season was the simple fact that it's difficult to find something you aren't looking for. Nothing like this had ever happened before. I had always time traveled to the exact same date, just a different year.

What made this time different? I tried to force my mind to remember the exact moment I had time traveled, but it was as if I was dragging myself kicking and screaming. Even now, the memory of seeing Seth and realizing he was dead was so intense that it set my heart to pounding. I fought the panic, but try as I might, I couldn't recall anything that had made this time travel unique from the others.

Who or what determined where I landed when time traveling? I had started in December and ended in June. Why? Why six months? Why this specific date?

Then it hit me. June. The numbers marking the date were in the corner of the screen when I'd used Wayne's computer. The significance of the date hadn't struck me until the clear memory of those numbers lit across my mind like a flashing neon light.

It was my wedding anniversary. I didn't know how or why, but I left the day my husband died and arrived on the anniversary of the day I had married him.

I felt tears threaten as I pulled into the parking lot of the ferry terminal. I stared straight ahead and took deep breaths, waiting for the burning behind my eyes to fade. Feeling my throat start to constrict, I began listing the elements of the periodic table. I didn't have time for a meltdown right now. I couldn't miss my one opportunity to get some answers from Wayne.

Somewhere around manganese, the distraction began to work. By the time I got to mercury at number 80, I was calm enough to leave the car and rush to get my ticket for the ferry.

By the time I'd figured out the vending machine and paid for my faire, the ferry was boarding. I hurried onto the ship, careful not to make eye contact with anyone.

Bypassing the large, double-decker cabin, I instead stood outside at the rail, pretending a fascination with the view across the bay. Though I'd taken a ferry a few years ago when I toured Alcatraz, this was the first time I'd been on the commuter ferry from Sausalito to San Francisco.

Taking a quick look around, I saw this wouldn't be a lightly attended trip across the bay. Thankfully, most of the passengers were inside with zombie-like focus on one of the TV screens that was mounted for optimal viewing. I really hoped that they were all seasoned commuters content to stay inside. Tourists would likely insist on crowding around the rail for the full Golden Gate Ferry experience.

A few minutes later, I was startled by the movement of the boat beneath my feet. We were moving already? Where was Wayne? I nervously glanced around, careful to keep my face down and away from anyone who happened to glance my way. Was Wayne on board?

About a hundred thoughts competed for my attention. Had something happened to prevent Wayne from meeting me? Maybe those looking for me had intercepted him. Or maybe Wayne had never really intended to meet me, but had planned to stand me up to get me away from him.

However, the more I thought about it, the more I realized Wayne wouldn't have intentionally stood me up. The box of costume supplies was proof that he planned to help me. If he wasn't here, then something had gone wrong.

I tried to calm my suddenly frantic thoughts, but if my enemies had intercepted Wayne, then they knew I was back in the area. What if I was headed straight for a trap?

The wind from the moving ferry whipped over and around me. My gaze bounced back and forth over the blue and white ship and two levels of her passengers, but I didn't know what I was looking for. It was too late to get off the boat. I looked back to see the ferry landing rapidly shrinking with our distance.

What was I going to do?

"Turn back around, Hannah," a voice hissed at my elbow. If anyone recognizes you, we'll both be dead!"

CHAPTER SIX

"DON'T look at me, Hannah!" Wayne ordered, staring toward the Golden Gate Bridge. "Pretend you're interested in the scenery. You don't know me."

I forced myself to keep my eyes straight ahead.

Though we were the only two people in this back corner of the ferry, the inside area was walled with windows on both levels. Wayne stood close enough to be heard yet not so close as if to appear we were more than fellow passengers.

"Who knows you're here?" Wayne asked, repeating the same first question he'd asked at the dealership.

"I already told you," I replied in frustration. "You are the only one."

I'd seen from my ticket that the trip across the bay would take approximately 25 minutes. He told me at the dealership that I couldn't contact him after this trip. That wasn't much time to cover ten years of history and develop a plan to make things right, especially when I had to answer the same stupid questions he had already asked.

"Hannah, I need to know how difficult it's going to be to keep you alive." Wayne's tone was businesslike and unemotional.

"You said you stayed at a hotel last night. Who did you have contact with? Who did you talk to or even make eye contact with? You are the most infamous woman of the past decade. Even an insignificant contact with someone means the potential that you were recognized."

I took deep breaths, tasting the salt-laced air and trying to focus past the knowledge that everyone in the country thought I was a modern-day villain. Wayne wanted his questions answered right now. Realistically, he was my only hope. Though so much had obviously changed in the past ten years, I had no choice but to trust this man who had repeatedly proven himself to be one of my best friends.

"It was late when I arrived at the hotel," I obediently reported. "I only spoke with the front desk clerk and Bryce Richardson, the college kid who gave me a ride this morning. I also spoke with a different clerk this morning. I didn't use my own name for the registration, and I paid with cash. No one even remotely seemed to recognize me."

"Then we might have a chance," Though the tension in Wayne's muscles visibly relaxed, his voice was still cautious. "I didn't know if you'd make it this far. With all of that security installed at Fort Baker Pier, it's almost as if Katherine knew you would show up there. Since I didn't know what happened that night ten-and-a-half years ago, I didn't know the details of your disappearance. I tried to be prepared in case you showed up one day, but after so much time, I'd begun to wonder if you hadn't time traveled but been killed."

"At this point, death seems preferable to what I'm going through," I whispered, not even sure my weak voice would carry to his ears across the breeze of the moving ferry.

"What happened, Hannah?" Wayne asked, his own voice laced with ten years of grief and uncertainty. "When we parted ways at the restaurant that night, you and Seth were going to get some evidence and deliver it to Mr. Smith. Then I heard nothing. For the next year, Abby and I had to pretend nothing had happened. Do you know how hard that was? You and Seth had left to save the world, but the Hannah and Seth of my current time had no idea that the world was in danger! Abby couldn't take it and told your parents, but then they had to keep the secret as well."

Wayne paused as an elderly woman passed close. Though he was silent for several seconds, his eyes never stopped moving. Even while he spoke, he was scanning every person on deck and focusing on faces visible through the windows.

At his actions, any sense of security vanished, and feelings of paranoia crowded me close.

The elderly woman walked to the railing several yards away, and Wayne continued his story. "Exactly one year later, I went with your parents and Abby to meet you at Fort Baker Pier, like Seth had instructed. When we got there, the gate was locked. At the time, it was just one of those long arm gates to prevent vehicles from entering. So your dad stayed with the car while your Mom, Abby, and I ducked under the gate.

"There was a car parked in the shadows down closer to the pier. We could see two people sitting inside, as if waiting. I stayed to watch them while your mom and Abby snuck down to the pier. Then I heard screaming. I ran down to the dock to find your mom and Abby in hysterics, you gone, and Seth dead."

Wayne hesitated and swallowed, as if unable to continue. Taking a deep breath, he finally met my eyes once again, his own gaze searching. "The things they say about you... I know they're not true. But I've never known what is true. What really happened that night?"

"I looked myself up on the Internet; I know what they say about me." Hoping to stop the constricting of my throat, I turned so the breeze hit my face directly. "You, more than anyone else, know how much was fabricated. I was not responsible for Jones-Stanton's harmful anti-depressant, and I didn't kill Seth."

Though everything in me rebelled against the thought of repeating the events from last night, I knew I had to do it for Wayne. Trying to keep emotion out of my voice, I worked to detach myself and simply recount the facts. "After we left you at the restaurant, we went to the Tomorrow Foundation and retrieved some files from Seth's work on the case. Katherine intercepted us. We got away, but only after a nightmarish chase through the city. We met Mr. Smith at the pier as planned and gave him the all of the evidence. Before we could leave, Katherine and another man with a gun showed up."

The breeze was cool, but not so cold that it could take the entire blame for the involuntary shiver that went through my body. "They had bribed our taxi driver into telling them where he had taken us. Seth tried to make a grab at Katherine, but the man with the gun shot. Seth fell, but I didn't know he'd been shot. He told me we had succeeded, that we had saved Abby and delivered the files. I realize now that he was trying to get me to time travel, and it worked. It wasn't until after I relaxed and we time traveled back to a year later that I realized he was injured. I ran for Seth's backpack, to try to find something to help him. But when I turned around…"

"He was dead." With slight impatience in his tone, Wayne finished the words I couldn't say. "And that's when you lost it and time traveled."

I nodded, though instant resentment flared at his insensitive tone. "I still don't understand," I said. I was tired of his questions and tired of his attitude.

Forgetting that we were supposed to maintain distance, I desperately reached out and gripped his arm, willing him to understand. "None of this was supposed to happen." How could anyone think I'd killed Seth? Mom and Abby saw me. They were running toward me, and I screamed at them to get you. They had to have seen me disappear. They were witnesses that I hadn't shot Seth—that I'd been trying to help him. And what about the gun? Without a weapon, how could they think I'd done it?"

"They found the gun, Hannah. It was right beside

Seth's body."

Shock like an electric wire ran from my head to my feet. "But how?"

"It had your fingerprints on it."

"That's impossible."

"It gets worse," Wayne looked out toward Alcatraz in the distance, and it was his turn to recount events, but he seemed to have no problem doing it in a stoic manner. "They have a witness who saw you buy the gun in his store a week before Seth was shot. He confessed that you'd paid a significant amount of money to keep the sale off the records. And then there's the speculation about the woman Seth had supposedly been having an affair with. Her identity was never revealed outside law enforcement, but all signs point that Katherine confessed to an affair with Seth and offered incriminating evidence about you. Of course, there is also proof implicating you as the mastermind behind the Jones-Stanton antidepressant scandal and attempted cover-up.

"There was a ridiculous amount of evidence, Hannah. Documents, videos, and emails left no room to question the facts that you murdered your husband and were solely responsible for a harmful drug that had injured and killed hundreds to thousands of people."

Dazed, I shook my head as whispers of denial left my lips repeatedly. "No. That's impossible."

Wayne shrugged. "It isn't when you have enough time and money, which was apparently not a problem for Katherine and Jones-Stanton."

Wayne's words paralyzed me with shock and fear, but what intensified those feelings to the point of being unbearable was the manner in which he'd delivered them. He wasn't angry. He wasn't disgusted. He didn't even have his normal, barely-concealed dislike when Katherine's name was mentioned. Instead, he was unemotional and defeated. There was no fight left in him. It was as if he had no will left and didn't even care anymore..

"But there was no gun!" I argued. "Seth was shot a year before; then we time traveled back to our correct time. The gun was with Katherine and the gunman a year before Seth's body was found on the pier."

"That just means Katherine had a year to prepare. She knew Seth had been shot, but then she probably saw both of you disappear. The next day, she would have seen Seth of that time walking around, completely healthy and ignorant of what had happened."

"But she doesn't know about my time traveling."

"She didn't then. But I imagine seeing you disappear would present a lot of questions in her mind. Katherine is smart. Remember, she also knew about you disappearing when you and Seth first met. She may not have figured everything out, but I'm sure she put enough together to cause her to take certain precautions. There was probably a lot of guess-work on her part; we don't know what all of her contingency plans were. But obviously, one of those plans included being ready to completely and elaborately frame you for everything if you and a mortally wounded Seth showed up at Fort Baker Pier a year later."

"But My mom and Abby were witnesses! They would have seen that there was no gun at the time Seth died and I disappeared. They would know it was planted!"

"They never had a chance to give any witness," Wayne whispered, his voice cracking with emotion for the first time. "Hannah, Abby and your parents are dead."

CHAPTER SEVEN

MY knees buckled. Wayne grabbed for me and kept me from hitting the deck. With his hands on either side of my ribs supporting my weight, he kept me at arm's length. He didn't try to hold me close in comfort, and he didn't try to soothe me with words. As soon as my feet were steady, he released me completely. I realized it would probably be a relief to him if emotion whisked me away in time travel again. At least then he wouldn't have to deal with me.

Suddenly, I was angry. I was angry at Katherine, at the faceless Jones-Stanton, and at God. I was even mad with Seth for dying and leaving me to face this alone.

Then all of that emotion focused, and I was ridiculously, red-hot furious with the man standing beside me. I turned toward him, put both my hands out, and pushed his chest. He took a step back in shock, and I pushed him again.

"You promised!" I seethed, balling up my fists. "You

said you would protect her! You promised Abby would be safe!"

As my small fists began pummeling Wayne's chest, he easily captured them and held them firmly in his hands.

"I know," he whispered brokenly.

Wayne abruptly straightened and looked around. Taken aback at the sudden change, I followed his gaze and quickly realized we were drawing curious stares from a few of the passengers loitering around the railing. A couple of faces in the windows were also focused intently our direction.

"Wayne, dear," an elderly lady appeared at Wayne's elbow and began incessantly tapping on his arm with her finger, trying to get his attention.. Her hair was snow white, which was in stark contrast to her orange Hawaiian print jacket.

She looked up over her glasses at the tall man. "Take my advice. Kiss that girl and be done with it. Life is too short to waste on quarrelling."

Wayne smiled down at her kindly. He reached over and gave her hand a gentle squeeze. "Thank you, Mrs. Swanson."

Apparently satisfied that her message had been delivered, Mrs. Swanson smiled, patted Wayne's hand and presumably left to bless other passengers with her bits of advice.

I raised my eyebrows. "I take it you come here often?" I asked, nodding toward Mrs. Swanson's retreating orange figure.

Wayne nodded. "If possible, I take the ferry every time I have to go into the city. I don't like the bridges."

"And Mrs. Swanson?"

"She is a regular," Wayne explained. "She frequently goes to visit her son. Of course, she prides herself on knowing her fellow regular travelers and dispensing unsolicited advice when needed."

As if realizing we were still positioned to be a main attraction for any other curious passengers, Wayne pulled me back toward the cabin area, where we could stand partially obstructed from view by the corner of the cabin box.

"Do you think it hasn't haunted me for the past ten years?" Though he still firmly held my hands, his eyes reflected misery and a plea for me to understand. "I know what I promised. And I tried. I kept her safe for a year, but on that same night that Seth died, I couldn't save her. I couldn't save any of them. I couldn't even save myself."

Wayne looked out back across the bay toward Sausalito. His whisper barely carried to my ears. "Everyone is dead. And sometimes I wish they would have finished the job with me."

That was something the Wayne I knew would never say.

Startled, I studied Wayne, really studied him for the first time since encountering this older version of my friend. Deep lines of grief trailed from his dull brown eyes. His forehead was creased with stress like parched, cracked ground. The light in his eyes and the ready grin I loved were gone, and by the look of the gray, haunted cast to his face, they had been gone for a long time.

Wayne was not prone to depression. He was a doer. If there was a problem, he might obsess to the point of driving himself and everyone else crazy coming up with a wacky, yet ingenious solution, but he would never throw in the towel and admit defeat.

"What happened?" I asked, the agonizing whisper covering my family as well as Wayne himself. Though the anger was gone from my voice, I couldn't mask the pain, but it was pain, not just over losing my parents and Abby, it was pain from losing Wayne too.

He struggled to answer, his throat working convulsively as he continued to stare out past the wake of the charging ferry.

"Maybe that's the worst part," Wayne finally replied. "I don't know what happened. I remember running down the dock. I remember kneeling over Seth and hearing Abby's screams and your mom's sobs. Seth wasn't breathing; he had no pulse. But I didn't want to believe he was dead. Before I could see where he was shot or start CPR, something happened. I don't know what, but my memories end in nothingness. I don't know if I was shot with some kind of tranquilizer or drugged in some way, but the next thing I know, I was waking up in a hospital three days later. Katherine was sitting beside my bed. She said, 'You are alive because of me.' Then she turned on the TV and handed me the remote. She nodded toward the TV, said 'It's over,' and left. I haven't seen her since."

"So that's it?" I asked sharply. "You just gave up because she said so? What about all the evidence against her and Jones-Stanton?"

"Hannah, every station on the TV was covering a massive manhunt—for you. Katherine was right. It was over, and there was nothing I could do. My life was the only thing Katherine left me. You were framed for murder, and I was framed as a low-level co-conspirator in the pharmaceutical scandal. The media ate up every false story like a pack of dogs after a bone. They had an entire fictitious story figured out before I was conscious. They said that I aided in your schemes, but turned on you after discovering the massive cover-up of the Jones-Stanton medication. Then you drugged me and left me for dead."

I shook my head, dazed with the twists in Wayne's story and my gut-level cry of denial that this had happened. "But how could they say that? There was no evidence!"

"That didn't matter." Wayne sighed wearily and cast an anxious glance toward the front of the boat. I knew he was trying to see how close we were to the San Francisco shore. "They manufactured whatever evidence they needed. They didn't even need me awake to completely rewrite my life. By day two of my drug-induced slumber, sources apparently reported that I struck a deal using my full cooperation as leverage. I woke on the third day to no jail time, but I also woke to no Tomorrow Foundation, no medical license, and no one who believed a word I said."

"And Abby and my parents?"

"The media called it an accident. The same night I woke, their car went off the road driving to Silver

Springs. The official report stated that Jackson Kraeger's blood alcohol level was over the legal limit."

"My dad didn't drink!" I insisted hoarsely.

Wayne shrugged. "The story that circulated through the media theorized that he was upset over the terrible things you had done, so he got drunk. Your family headed to Silver Springs to try to escape the media, but they never made it. Open bottles of alcohol were found in the car."

"That's impossible"

"What are you not understanding, Hannah?" Frustration dripped from his voice. "It doesn't matter if your dad never had a drop of alcohol in his life! It was a set up."

"I realize that!" I said, my own frustration matching his. "I understand that it was a massive, evil, intricate, beautiful frame-job that Katherine probably spent a year planning for. But all of this," I waved my hands to indicate Wayne and everything else around me, "shouldn't have happened. Tom tried to kill Abby. I saw Seth hand the files to Mr. Smith. It was supposed to be over that night ten years ago. Tom and Katherine were supposed to go to jail, Jones-Stanton was to be stopped and turned in to the authorities, and so many lives should have been saved by exposing the truth of that anti-depressant."

"Come on, Hannah! Some of this you should be figuring out on your own! Abby never got to file charges against Tom. She had no evidence. Besides, she had to be careful not to reveal too much about how you and Seth rescued her. I'm sure saying that two time travelers from the future came to rescue her from her psychotic, murderous husband wouldn't have gone very well in court."

"Ladies and Gentlemen," the loudspeaker behind me suddenly blared.

My heart leapt, and my body followed. Had they discovered that I was on board?

Wayne gripped my forearm tightly, trying to keep me calm.

In a calm, relaxed, though jarringly loud voice, the loudspeaker continued belching out its announcement. "Some of you may have noticed that our speed has slowed. We are currently having some mild engine difficulties. Nothing dangerous, I assure you. We just have to keep our speed below normal. Our ferries were recently upgraded to use a greener fuel, and that has apparently left us with some unforeseen complications. We will be arriving in San Francisco later than scheduled. I apologize for the delay and any difficulties it may cause with your plans. Please enjoy the beautiful views as we finish our journey across the bay."

"That's good, right?" I said. "We should have a little more time now."

Wayne grimaced. "Except I'll be late to work at the car show."

Despite Wayne's sour attitude, I was going to use every extra minute we had. I was going to get answers. I needed to know what had gone wrong and how to set things right.

"What about Mr. Smith?" I threw out, desperate to believe that all of our efforts hadn't been in vain. "He was the one who had all of the evidence and was going to turn it in."

Wayne shook his head. "I never saw or heard from Mr. Smith ever again. I don't know what happened. Maybe Katherine and her cronies got to him too. For that entire year between when you saved Abby and when you showed back up at Fort Baker Pier, we kept waiting for something to happen. I figured either the Jones-Stanton scandal would go public or if you and Seth hadn't succeeded with the evidence, then Katherine and Tom would come after us and the other Seth and Hannah who knew nothing about what had happened. We lived in fear, yet we never developed a good plan for what to do if Katherine confronted us and your time traveling became the issue we couldn't avoid. But nothing happened. Nothing at all. Then in one night, everything happened, and I lost it all."

Wayne looked at me, his brown eyes dull and resigned. "You need to accept it, Hannah. Katherine won, and there is nothing you can do about it. If you're lucky, you will do like me and escape with your life."

"That is not acceptable." I gritted out fiercely. "She has not won! I will fix this!"

"Hannah, if you go after Katherine, you do it alone. I won't help you." Wayne held his hands up, showing he wanted nothing to do with me.

"I didn't mean I wanted to fix it *now*. I've done it

before; I can do it again. There are two ways for me to time travel. Relaxing may not ever be an option for me again, but if I scare myself like last time… I may be able to go back to a specific time. I can make this right."

"Isn't that what caused this mess in the first place?" The corner of Wayne's mouth lifted in scorn. "You didn't like what time had done, so you decided to change it. That didn't seem to work out well, did it?"

"If I do nothing, then Seth and everyone else will have died for nothing!" My eyes burned and the fierce tone of my voice shook with desperation. "I can't live with that."

"I don't think that will be a problem." Instead of matching my emotion, Wayne lazily leaned against the side of the cabin and responded as if remarking on the weather. "You'll be dead long before you have the chance to change anything."

"Then what would you have me do, Wayne?" I burst angrily, tears finally cresting and running down my cheeks.

Wayne replied calmly, "Kiss and make up."

CHAPTER EIGHT

"WH-AT?" I stumbled, shaking my head in confusion.

"If you look around, Hannah, we are once again the primary entertainment for a large number of passengers with nothing to do. We don't want them getting too curious or thinking we're more than just an arguing couple. I think we need to play the part and take Mrs. Swanson's advice to kiss and make up."

Wayne took a step toward me.

I took a step back, which landed me with my back against the cabin wall. "But I'm married!"

"No, you were married. Your husband has been dead for ten years now."

"But I—"

Wayne's lips on mine cut off my protest. I was so startled that I couldn't think. Wayne had said to play the part, but his warm, firm lips moving against mine felt all-too real. It almost seemed as if his kiss was a mirror for the entirety of our relationship.

At first it was almost mechanical, like two friends going through the motions for a play. I had only ever felt a deep friendship for Wayne, but I knew he had felt something much more for me. What started out as his friendly kiss suddenly caught fire and morphed into something else entirely.

Wayne's mouth pulsated over mine hungrily. Stunned, I couldn't breathe, let alone respond. I put my hands against his chest to push him away, but the contact only seemed to encourage him. I was in the corner and had nowhere to go as his arms came around me. His hands moved over my back and slid up to the base of my neck. My hat came off. His hands slipped under the scarves, loosening my hair for him to tangle his fingers. He pulled me ever closer, his passion intensifying. I couldn't breathe.

I don't know the moment it happened, but right as his kiss was communicating a deep and passionate love, it subtly began translating something else too. His hands released their hold around me, but lifted to brace on either side of the corner, trapping me. His lips, which had been caressing, gradually became more harsh and demanding. They crushed mine, hurting in their ferocity. I felt anger and even tinges of hatred. I still felt his attraction and love for me, but it was a strange, agonizing mix with severe anger.

Then, it was as if Wayne suddenly came to his senses. One second he was lost in his emotions, the next those emotions disappeared as if they'd never existed.

What was left was a paint-by-numbers kiss. It was all form and no emotion. His hands dropped again and slowly draped around me like wet noodles. After two last, lingering seconds with his lip pressed woodenly against mine, he pulled his arms away and stepped back.

"Now smile and pretend to be relieved. We just made-up after an epic fight."

Though he was trying to appear calm and unaffected, I saw a slight tremor in his hands, and he wouldn't look me in the eye.

I obediently pasted on a make-believe smile, but the accompanying look of relief was completely genuine.

Wayne's gaze skimmed me, and his eyes widened in panic. "Fix your hair!"

I raised my hand to feel my hair sticking out of the wrapped scarves. Wayne moved close, trying to block the view of any audience while I hurriedly worked to repair the damage. I pulled the hair back up, rewrapped it with the end of the scarf, and stuck the hat back on top. Finished, I looked up at Wayne. Instead of retreating, his face stayed close, right by my shoulder. Having him so near made me extremely nervous, but as I hesitantly met his eyes, I saw only guilt and sorrow as he gazed down at me.

"Hannah, I…"

"It's okay, Wayne." I said quickly. I could hear the apology in his voice and see it on his face, but I also knew he had as much desire to talk about that kiss as I did. If I could just find a way to change things, then I could make it so that everything, including that kiss would never happen. Then I would be the only one with that memory, and I could bury it forever.

Wayne nodded and backed up.

"Wayne," I whispered, desperate to take advantage of his moment of vulnerability. "If you just help me, I can make it so the past ten years never existed. I just have to have good timing." I stood up straighter, trying to appear more confident and resolute than I felt while attempting to conceal how shaken-up I was.

Wayne sighed. "That may not be possible." His tone was flat, yet his eyes pierced me with intensity. "Katherine knows."

I nodded and gave a slight shrug. "I realize there's a very good chance Katherine has guessed some of my story; she may even suspect about my time traveling. After all, she's smart. But none of that will matter. She can't know everything. Besides, I'll go back to a point when she hasn't figured things out."

"But she *can* know everything! That's what I'm talking about." Wayne let out a frustrated breath. "I told you that I was unconscious for three days after Seth died. When I woke, Abby and your parents had just died that day. So what happened to them between the time when I was captured and when they died? It was three days, Hannah."

My eyes widened as the realization hit. "You don't think…?" I suddenly felt sick and hurried to the side of the boat. I held my face into the wind while trying to capture deep, calming breaths of the cool air moving past.

Wayne had followed, but was silently waiting at my

elbow.

"So you think Katherine tortured my family for information," I finally said, trying to keep the gut-wrenching emotion out of my voice.

"I don't know," Wayne said quietly. "I promised you that I'd take care of Abby, and I wasn't able to keep that promise. But that guilt in no way compares to what I feel at the thought of what she and your parents possibly went through in those three days. When I woke, Katherine asked me nothing. No questions at all. She didn't need to."

I lifted my gaze to meet his own personal torture reflected in his eyes.

Then, like a window blind being drawn, his emotions fell behind a mask, and he became a soldier stoically giving a report to his commanding officer. "Since I was apprehended, it's unlikely that they escaped the dock either. That means there are three days unaccounted for. I have to at least consider the possibility that they were interrogated in some way and then disposed of. I don't think either one of us buys the story of a drunken accident."

"Help me fix it, Wayne." I breathed desperately, reaching out to grab his hand in mine. "All of it. I can go back to before Katherine knew anything. I can…"

"Hannah, it won't work. Katherine wouldn't have been satisfied until she knew everything about you. And she's spent the last ten years being very satisfied. She knows everything, and she's had years to plan. She's been waiting for you. You don't have enough, or any, control of your time travel. If you try to fix this, you're going to make it worse."

"How can things possibly be worse?"

"Trust me, it can always get worse. I think I've sacrificed enough for the cause."

"I know you have, Wayne. But that's part of what I need to fix."

"Hannah, I already told you I can't help you. I won't help you." Wayne's mouth was set in a straight line as he gritted out the words.

It was that moment that I realized I didn't know this man.

I looked at him, really looked at him, as if seeing Wayne Hawkins for the first time. Yes, there were remnants of the man I had known: he was the same height, and his eyes were the same brown hue. But other than the faint physical features that age hadn't yet erased, I didn't recognize him.

The Wayne Hawkins that I had known was my friend, and more than that; he'd been at least half-way in love with me since the first time we'd met. Wayne was loyal, funny, and fearless. He would always protect, especially me, and never shy away from a fight. His deep sense of integrity would never allow him to compromise, and his stubborn determination would never allow him to give up, no matter what the cost to him personally.

I grasped at anything that might make him remember who he was. "Wayne, you're the one who has always encouraged me to embrace my ability to time travel.

You've said God gave it to me with a purpose in mind."

"I was an idiot," he said flatly. "Or maybe we all were. But you can't blame this on me or God, Hannah. As I recall, you didn't consult anyone but yourself when you decided to go back and save Abby. Every one of your trips before that had been accidental. The moment you decided to purposely screw with time, you destroyed what should have happened and ruined everyone's lives in the process."

I flinched at his words, as if they were a physical force. When exactly was that moment? As Wayne said, had I ruined everything with my decision to save Abby, or had it been much earlier? Had a simple note written on a napkin to Seth McAllister so many years ago been the catalyst to change history and create this alternate, nightmarish reality?

Wayne's voice pinned me relentlessly. "After everything that has happened, you really think you're smart and capable enough to give it another go?

"No, I'm not," I flung out desperately. "I can't do this on my own. I know I don't deserve it. I know these past ten years have been awful in a way that I can't imagine. But you're my friend. I need you. If for no other reason than for the way you once felt about me, please help me now."

"All of that is gone now, Hannah. You killed it along with everything else of value in your life." Wayne's voice was as dead as his words. His eyes held no emotion; his expression conveyed no compassion.

I met those unfamiliar brown eyes. Unable to hide the

hurt and accusation, I broke the connection and looked away.

"Don't look at me like that, Hannah." Wayne growled lowly. "You're acting as if I'm the villain. Do you even realize that I'm risking my life by simply speaking to you? I won't help the way you want me to, but I'm also not collecting the reward for your apprehension. I have a plan to get you out of the country. I will give you all the information you'll need, but whether you use it will be your decision. Either way, when this ferry docks, I'm done. You will go your way, and I will head to work at the car show in the city. I never want to see you or hear from you again."

I nodded my acceptance even as I worked to control the burning sensation behind my eyes. Wayne Hawkins was a broken man. His will to fight had been crushed like the butt of a cigarette. I couldn't expect him to think and behave like the Wayne I had known. That man no longer existed. He was as dead as Seth. And also just like Seth, his death was my fault.

"Go to the docks across the bay in Richmond and ask for Jake Hopper. Tell him I sent you, and he'll know what to do. I saved his daughter's life, so he owes me and is prepared with the plan. He makes frequent runs down to Mexico in his ship. He will provide the necessary documents, transportation, and some cash, but after you leave his ship, you're on your own."

My mind whirled as I tried to keep up with Wayne's instructions. He had obviously taken a huge risk and put a lot of effort into developing a plan for my escape. But no matter what he said, I just didn't think I could do it. I couldn't give up. I couldn't abandon all possibility of saving Seth and my family. I had no desire to live out the rest of my days stuck in this screwed up timeline in Mexico. If I ever did manage to time travel again, then I wouldn't be where I could have a chance to change things.

Despite everything, I wasn't broken yet. While there was still breath in me, I had to fight to fix this mess I'd created.

However, at this point, I had no idea how to do that, especially with no help.

"Now all of this hinges on you not being recognized before you reach the docks," Wayne said with furrowed brow. "If you are, the bridges will be shut down and the entire city will be on the manhunt of the century. There's no way you'll escape."

Wayne paused, reading my face. "You think I'm exaggerating. I'm not. Katherine Colson is the governor."

"The governor?" I echoed as chills called goose bumps to the surface of my skin.

"Yes, and a very popular governor at that. She's practically royalty. She can do no wrong in the eyes of the public. Her word is law. And the worst part is, she's still young. Who knows what she will achieve in the future?

Immediately, a memory unfolded like a scroll in front of my mind. I had time traveled to the future for the first time and was watching a TV monitor in the waiting room of Intrepid research facility. On the screen was the president of the United States, and she bore a striking resemblance to Katherine.

I felt sick to my stomach. But it wasn't caused by the simple thought of Katherine in positions of power; I felt sick with the certainty that I was the one who had to stop her.

"Tell me about this kid you spoke to," Wayne was saying. "You said his name was Bryce Richardson? If he recognized you, then you have no chance."

I tried to refocus on Wayne. I needed to pretend to go along with his plan. He didn't need to know that I wouldn't use it. After the ferry docked, he could go on his way, knowing that he had done everything he could for me. I owed him at least that.

"Bryce didn't know me," I assured. "He said I looked familiar, but at the time, I thought he was just hitting on me.

Wayne winced. "That's not good. That means he recognized you; he just can't remember from where. He's undoubtedly seen your picture, and when he connects the two in his mind, he'll report you. Our only chance is to try to get you to Mexico before that happens. Once Katherine and her cronies know you're in the area, they'll come looking for me. I'm your only associate left alive. They'll know you made contact."

I shook my head. "I was careful. I had Bryce drop me off several blocks from your work so he wouldn't see where I went."

"That doesn't matter. It was close enough. They'll still know you came to me. I'm sure they'll sweep my office for prints and everything. I tried to wipe all surfaces down right before I came to the ferry, but it's still very likely they'll find evidence of your presence."

Alarm shot through me. "Wayne, you need to go to Mexico too! They'll come after you!"

"No, I'll stay and stall long enough to make sure you're thoroughly lost in Mexico."

"You don't have to do that, Wayne! I think I already bought us a little time."

At his questioning look, I rushed to explain. "I used your computer to find out what had happened the past 10 years, but I also deleted the history and planted a false trail. I made it appear like I was looking up an old friend from high school. They'll think I'm headed to her house up north. I'm sure that wild goose chase will give you enough time to make a run for Mexico."

"I don't think that's going to matter," Wayne said woodenly, staring at something beyond my left shoulder. "Is Bryce Richardson a punk rich kid with brown hair?"

"Yes," I answered cautiously. With sudden dread, I turned to follow Wayne's gaze.

Through the glass of the cabin, I saw the TV mounted overhead in optimal position for passenger viewing. On the TV was a news report. On the news report was an obviously upset Bryce Richardson.

A picture of a serious, red-haired, young woman flashed on the screen.

It was me.

CHAPTER NINE

BRYCE had remembered. As I watched his animated movements while being interviewed, I realized he was likely spinning fantastic stories of how I hijacked his car and made him drive me to downtown Sausalito.

Wayne spoke with quiet urgency. "They'll be coming for me."

"But the ferry is running late! They could be waiting for you when we dock!"

"The delay can work to our advantage," Wayne said, trying to look around the side of the ferry to catch a glimpse of the approaching pier. "According to my itinerary, I should already be at the car show. If they are trying to find me, they'll look there first. When I'm not there, they'll try to retrace my movements and check the ferry. There won't be much time, but you may be able to escape before they apprehend me."

Both of us leaned over the railing, but neither he nor I

could see if police or other officials were waiting on the rapidly approaching pier.

"Hannah, assuming they don't block the exit, you have to be one of the first off the ferry." Wayne turned toward me, his serious eyes squarely meeting mine and communicating the vital importance of his words. "It's your only chance. I'll wait at the back and try to stall. Even with the delay, it won't take them long to locate me."

"But you have to escape, too," I insisted. "They will know you've seen me. If I have time to escape, then you have time."

Wayne shook his head. "Don't worry about me. Just get yourself away from here. Mexico is not an option now. I'm sorry, Hannah. Apparently my brilliant plan wasn't so brilliant after all."

Time was running out. A few passengers were already milling toward the front of the ferry.

Unnerved, I reached out and gripped his hand. "But they'll question you! After what they did to Abby and my family…"

"I can't be forced to give answers I don't have," Wayne said, squeezing my hand gently. "I don't know where you're going. I don't even know how you'll survive the next few hours. I knew the risks, Hannah. My life has been wrapped up with yours since the moment we met. Despite everything, they were risks I had to take."

His face was sad, but his sincerity shone through. For just a moment, those chocolate brown eyes were the same ones that belonged to my friend. Maybe I'd been wrong about Wayne. Maybe he hadn't changed as much as I'd thought. He was sacrificing himself for me. He was doing it with the full knowledge that he may be tortured or killed, and he was doing it bravely and willingly. Even though I had ruined his life, he was still saving me and asking for nothing in return.

"I'll fix it, Wayne," I whispered. "I promise."

Even as the words escaped my lips, I wished I could snatch them back. I'd heard those two little words before.

Wayne's mouth twitched in a sad smile of irony. "Be careful. Sometimes promises can't be kept no matter how hard you try."

Looking out at the water, I saw other ships bearing the Golden Gate Ferry colors lined up at attention. We were getting close.

"Wayne, I…" I wanted to say 'thank you.' I wanted to tell him with certainty that I would change time so this event would never happen. But I couldn't draw the words out of my soul.

"Go." Wayne said firmly.

I nodded and bit my lip, trying to keep the tears of guilt and self-hatred from rolling down my cheeks. Everything in me protested that this was wrong. I should not leave Wayne to sacrifice himself.

But instead, I walked away.

As the ferry slowly nosed up to the pier, I shot a quick glance back over my shoulder to see Wayne standing near a woman about my height. I realized he was trying to provide a decoy. If the authorities were expecting to find Hannah McAllister with Wayne, hopefully it would buy me some extra time and a little less scrutiny if they initially guessed the other woman to be me.

As the ferry came to a stop, I covertly studied the dock. There were only a few men scattered around, each in a blue uniform identifying him as an employee of the Golden Gate Ferry.

The coast was clear, and even that made me nervous. Was it a trap? Were they lying in wait to apprehend me? My heart pounded and my muscles tightened with tension.

The plank was lowered, and I crowded forward. I didn't want to attract attention by being the first off the boat, but I couldn't be pushed back in the shuffle of passengers trying to disembark.

Thankfully, I managed to hold my position, allowing only two people ahead of me.

The instant my feet hit the dock, I heard shouting.

"Stop! Don't let anyone off the ferry!"

Police and men in suits were running up the pier. Passengers froze, momentarily paralyzed by the authoritative command.

"Everyone stay where you are!"

As the authorities descended in a jumble of confusion, I weaved past the two spooked passengers in front of me. I kept moving forward, keeping my head down and refusing to make eye contact as I pushed past the uniforms of police and ferry personnel trying to sort out the chaos.

I passed the last official. He didn't even look my direction. Everyone was behind me.

My steps quickened along with my agitated breathing.

Twenty more feet and I'd reach the gate to the ferry terminal.

One step… Two… So close!

"Stop!"

I heard the shout. I knew they had seen me, but I moved faster, not acknowledging the call or glancing back over my shoulder.

"Stop!" The call came again. "You can't leave!"

At the sound of footsteps behind me, I took off.

People were crowded around the base of the pier, waiting to board the ferry for the return trip. I brushed past the gate and dodged my way through the crowd, bumping and jostling people in my haste.

"Stop her!"

At the command, hands descended, grabbing at me. Someone latched onto my backpack, yanking me back.

I jabbed my elbow back, connecting with something solid.

The grip released.

I jerked my arms away, flinging myself forward faster than the shout could reach and organize an effective ambush.

My breathing was erratic and there was a loud ringing in my ears, but I kept running. I made it past the ferry self-pay stations and past the entrance to the ferry terminal. As I reached the crowded sidewalk, I turned left. I repeatedly ran into people who weren't fast enough getting out of the way. Seth's heavy backpack bounced against my spine. I might be able to sprint faster without it, but I refused to abandon it.

Without apology, I stumbled away to the tune of more angry shouts and colorful language trailing behind me. By the sound of the commotion in my wake, I knew they were still after me. Others began to take up the call.

"Stop that woman! Grab her! Don't let her get away!"

I chanced a glance behind me and plowed into something large and solid. The air knocked from my lungs. I struggled to breathe and regain my balance. Through my swirling vision, I saw that I'd run into a street performer who was dressed and painted in silver from head to toe.

At the impact, the human statue broke, becoming a very angry man. Yelling and cursing, he pushed me back hard.

I fell. Twisting my ankle badly, I landed in a heap on the sidewalk. Pain sliced through my ankle.

The man/statue was still shouting at me, and I knew I had only seconds before my pursuers drug me up off the cement and into their custody.

Fueled by sheer panic, I pulled myself up. My eyes lit

on a nearby alley, and I stumbled inside.

With the silver man's attention momentarily diverted by my oncoming posse, I didn't know if he saw me enter the alley. But I had to get away before my enemies stopped to look which direction I'd gone.

Adrenaline numbed the pain as I forced my feet into a jog, Another alley intersected this one, so I turned right. At the next alley intersection, I turned right again. I ran steadily for another five minutes, not stopping, just turning a different direction at every alley I came to and getting thoroughly lost in the labyrinth. Realizing that I hadn't heard any sound of pursuit since I'd entered the alleys, I finally slowed to a walk.

Then the pain hit. Sharp spikes of white-hot agony radiated up from my already throbbing ankle. I turned one more corner and could not go any further. I had no idea where I was, but I could see that this particular alley ended at a street.

I stumbled forward and fell in a heap behind the dumpster placed near the entrance to the alley.

I braced my ankle on my other knee. Moaning, I held it and rocked back and forth in agony. I don't know at what point I started crying, but I suddenly realized I was sobbing and not just from the physical pain. I felt an ache down to the core of my being, starting in my chest and radiated through every cell in my body. The intense love I had felt for Seth, Abby, and my parents could now only be translated as intense grief.

"How could God let this happen? Everyone I loved in life was dead and had been dead for the past ten years. I didn't think God was supposed to let evil prosper, but he had! The bad guys had won and were now in such positions of power that I had no hope of going against such a Goliath.

Wayne was right, I wouldn't last even a few hours with the entire country searching for me. I had nowhere to go. No one to help me. Everyone who knew about my time traveling was dead or unable to help.

Was this my punishment? To have everything taken away? To have the people I loved tortured and then forever silenced? I hadn't sought God's approval when I'd sent myself on a mission to save Abby, but I'd been motivated by love—a deep love for my sister.

Now God had taken everyone away and abandoned me. I was sitting by a dumpster with a badly sprained ankle. I didn't know where to go or what to do to survive the next few hours, let alone attempt to set things right. I had no one. And I had no idea even where I was.

In the midst of my sobbing, I gradually became aware of the cold seeping from the concrete to my rear end, the poky brick at my back biting into my spine, and the nauseating smell of garbage. I didn't know where to place my next footstep, but I knew I couldn't stay here.

I wiped my eyes with the collar of my trench-coat, trying to dry some of the watery blur from my vision. Looking down, I saw makeup now smeared all over the collar. Tears filled my eyes once again as I realized I may have just destroyed my disguise.

What a stupid thing to do! I thought, angry with myself. Crying did me absolutely no good. It didn't change the situation. Obviously, there wasn't anyone around who cared whether I lived or died, let alone whether I was stuck in an alleyway hurt and sobbing.

I couldn't stay here. It wouldn't take my enemies long to mount a thorough search of the area. They would know I hadn't gone far. I needed to know where I was and figure out how to escape to somewhere I couldn't be found. And of course, I also had the pressing needs of food and shelter, and some way to protect myself would be a plus as well. Unfortunately, I couldn't imagine how any of that that would be possible with cameras everywhere and my face likely plastered over every news and internet source around the country.

Still hiccupping sobs, I inched away from the wall and crawled until I could peek my head around the large, stinky dumpster. Cars drove past on the narrow street edged with multi-storied buildings standing tall and close like cereal boxes in the typical style of San Francisco. I scanned my limited field of view for something that seemed familiar or would give me a clue to an exact location. My tear-blurred eyes focused on a small ornate sign on the ground floor of one of the buildings.

It read 'Art Gallery.'

At the sight of the simple words, I ducked my head and crawled back to the wall where I curled into the fetal position. I recognized the sign. I knew exactly where I was.

CHAPTER TEN

KNOWLEDGE of my location did me no good. I still had no idea what to do, and now I had no choice but to let the tears flow once again as I lost myself in the memory of when I had first seen that sign.

It was when Abby had been dead for three months.

Though I had been trying to plot my rescue attempt, I was still depressed and plagued with what ifs. What if I didn't save her? At the moment, she was gone, and there was an aching void in my life.

I had known Seth was worried about me. He kept trying to do things to cheer me up. He wanted to go on a trip somewhere, but I refused. I wished I could pull myself out of the depression, at least for Seth's sake, but I couldn't. It was hard on him, but the guilt from straining my husband and our relationship only added to my depression.

That was why, when Seth eagerly announced he had a

surprise for me, I decided to humor him. I hated surprises. But he looked like a little boy handing me a present that he'd made himself, and I couldn't kill the joyful anticipation on his face no matter how much I just wanted him to leave me alone.

Without any clues to our destination, Seth drove me to a parking garage near downtown San Francisco. I drew the line when he wanted to blindfold me for what he said was a short walk. Hand in hand Seth led me down the sidewalk and then stopped below a small, old-fashioned sign labeled 'Art Gallery.'

At my questioning look, Seth said, "This is Deshaunds Art Gallery. It is one of the most respected galleries in the city."

Without waiting for a response, Seth led me inside.

I groaned inwardly. It was sweet of Seth to try to plan an activity I would like, but I really wasn't in the mood to look at art. The thought of having to feign interest in countless paintings was more than I could bear.

The gallery was larger than it appeared on the outside and arranged tastefully in separate rooms that were expertly decorated and lighted to provide maximum appeal for the art. It was a beautiful gallery, one I would have loved to wander through prior to Abby's death.

Seth led me through several rooms, as if he wanted me to see something specific. The place was empty except for one lady, who I assumed was the proprietor. She was 50ish and dressed smartly in business attire. She nodded at Seth in recognition as we passed, almost as if she'd been expecting us and had already been informed of the plan.

A hint of alarm shot through me. He better not have bought anything! I clearly remembered Seth and Wayne's suggestions for decorating the offices of the Tomorrow Foundation, specifically their insistence on the safe over the toilet. I in no way trusted my husband's taste!

Seth led me to a set of frames illuminated by subtle spotlights in the darkened room. He stopped, and I looked up at him, questioning why we were here. At his expectant look in return, I gathered he wanted me to look at the art.

I obediently looked at the small frames grouped as a collection on the wall and felt my heart drop to my feet.

Each frame held a small drawing of intricately detailed flowers, landscapes, or abstract curlicues each done on a napkin. A small plaque labeled the work with my name.

My napkin art.

I turned and pierced Seth with a look of shock, hurt, and anger. Before his face could register surprise at my reaction, I spun around and walked quickly back toward the front of the gallery. I was leaving.

"Hannah, wait!" Seth called, hurrying to catch up with me.

I ignored him and kept walking. But before I could make it out the door, Seth cut me off, maneuvering around me to block my way. He put his hands on my shoulders, forcing me to stop.

"Hannah, please don't do this. Don't shut me out.

Tell me what's wrong. What did I do?"

"You really don't know, Seth?" I whispered fiercely. If we were home, my voice would have undoubtedly been raised. But this gallery had an atmosphere that, like a library, seemed to demand that only whispers intrude upon the silence. "You took *my* napkins and put them in a gallery without my permission!"

"Technically, they were *my* napkins," Seth replied cautiously. "You either gave them to me or I picked them up when you left them for the trash. They were mine to do with as I wished, and I wished for others to be able to see and appreciate your work as I do."

"But they're napkins!" I protested. "You can't even term them art. They are doodles done on pieces of trash! I didn't want other people to see them, and I didn't want my name being propped there like they're something to be proud of."

Seth's eyes flashed understanding, and I knew he suddenly realized that my overwhelming emotions were embarrassment and insecurity.

"Hannah, come here," Seth said softly.

At the gentle love in his eyes, I reluctantly allowed him to lead me back through the gallery to the wall of framed napkins.

I saw the proprietor out of the corner of my eye as she slipped away into another room. She had undoubtedly heard our exchange at the front of the gallery, which only added to my embarrassment.

"Hannah, look at your work," Seth said softly,

wrapping his arms around me from behind. "Look at the detail. Look at the stark contrast of the black ink on the white background. Think about the incongruity of having a picture so exquisite on something that is normally wadded up and thrown away. Hannah, your work is beautiful."

"Seth, you know my doodling is a nervous habit," I said quietly, still trying to adjust to the sight of my work on display. "I never drew them to be art or even to be shared. They are an outlet of emotion for me. I only gave them to you because you liked them, but I never intended anyone but you to see them or appreciate them."

I stepped out of Seth's embrace and stepped forward. There was only one napkin that had words, and I lifted my finger to point to it. "That napkin is the one I had Wayne give to you. You waited five years for me because of that flimsy little message." I pointed to another frame. "This is the one I drew on our honeymoon. It was a few days after I time traveled, and we were sitting at dinner watching the sunset."

I turned back to my husband. "Seth, these are personal. They are full of the raw emotions I was feeling at the time I doodled them. The thought of other people seeing them terrifies me, not only because they're napkins, but because they make me feel vulnerable. They tell my story. They aren't a completed work of art; they are the working out of my own issues."

"That's where you're wrong, Hannah. They are art. How can you be such a wonderful artist and not consciously realize that art is personal? That's what makes it special, if it can communicate a fraction of emotion as a message from its creator."

"But they're napkins," I protested yet again. "How much did you have to pay to bribe the owner to display doodled napkins?"

"You've obviously not looked around, Hannah. This gallery appreciates the unusual in the world of art. I paid nothing. The owner was actually very excited to display your work; she felt the contrast of the beauty on something as disposable as a napkin was a powerful message. The gallery here will be selling lithograph versions of the napkins, but we will retain full ownership of the originals." Seth chuckled lightly. "The owner had a little difficulty with the printing. She insisted that even the copies be done on napkins."

"Seth, please don't flatter me. I know your family has connections. You and your mom probably pulled a bunch of strings to get these napkins onto this wall. I've told you before that I wanted to do this on my own. I didn't want any preferential treatment. And I certainly didn't want to be known for this." I waved my hand in a circle, indicating everything on the wall.

"Hannah, you did do it on your own. Yes, my mom got me an appointment, but it in no way guaranteed preferred treatment. The gallery owner loved the idea and the work itself. You got here on your own merits."

"Yes, and doodles on napkins will surely earn me lots of credibility."

"Sweetheart, you've always wanted to explore the possibility of making a name for yourself as an artist, but you've never really pursued it. And I blame myself."

My eyes opened wide in surprise, and instant denial leapt to my lips.

Seth held up his hand to stop me. "I pushed you to get your Master's degree in Chemistry. I asked you to help out at the Tomorrow Foundation. But I never intended for you to give up on your art. You say these aren't real art, but you haven't worked on anything else in a very long time. I would have loved to also bring a full-sized drawing or painting, but there wasn't anything else. You did that one painting at Stowe Lake when you time traveled last. I tried repeatedly to get you to put the finishing touches on that one, but it hasn't happened. I thought that if I was able to get your napkin art into a gallery, you might gain some confidence in yourself and finish that painting, and the one after that, and the one after that."

I turned and looked once again at the framed napkins. I tried to see the display without my bias and view it as someone who was seeing it for the first time.

The display itself was arranged very tastefully. Like Seth had said, the black ink on the white background could be considered very striking. And, with a little work, I could imagine someone might actually appreciate the beauty of such intricate drawings on something so temporal and disposable.

I felt a tiny flicker of hope. Maybe my napkin art wasn't something to be embarrassed about. I didn't like the idea of branding myself the 'napkin lady,' but maybe the napkins could at least give me a foot in the door. With something already accepted by a respected gallery, maybe I could do other drawings or paintings that may also be acceptable.

"I'm sorry, Hannah," Seth whispered, regret in his tone. "I should have asked your permission. But I was afraid you'd never agree. Then I got the idea of surprising you with it, and well, you know I have a weakness for a good surprise. However, from your reaction, I doubt you would label it as 'good.'"

I reached out, took his hand, and gently wove my fingers through his. "I'm warming up to it," I said, somewhat reluctantly.

Unfortunately, that was all the encouragement Seth needed. His blue-green eyes sparkled, and his face split in a grin that called his dimples out to perform.

I shouldn't have mentioned anything. Where surprises were concerned, if you gave Seth an inch, he'd take a mile. I'd just doomed myself to a great deal more Seth McAllister specials.

"This is for you," Seth said, picking up a small frame from a little decorative stand nearby.

"I'm not an artist," Seth said, "but I hope you like it." Acting uncharacteristically hesitant, Seth shyly handed me the frame.

It was identical to those on the wall and likewise had a napkin inside. But the napkin wasn't one of mine. It had no doodles. Instead, it had a bunch of dates written in small, black letters and scattered all around. The first date in the upper left corner leapt out at me. That date was seared into my memory as the day my life changed forever. It was the date I'd first time traveled to. It was the day I'd saved the entire Lawson family and met a charming medical student named Seth McAllister.

Having identified the one date, my gaze slid over the rest of the numbers, recognizing other significant days in my life since then. There was the first Christmas we spent together, the day I time traveled back from the future and almost died, the day Seth proposed, our wedding day, and the day Abby died.

In the center were the words:

I have loved you in every time, and will love you in all times to come.

Tears filled my eyes. I looked up to find such a look of vulnerability on my husband's face. Such a sweet, romantic man! All thoughts of being upset with him over his surprise vanished liked they'd never existed.

I set the frame gently back on the little table, put my hands on either side of Seth's face, and drew him down to where I could trail soft kisses along his jawline. Oh, how I loved this man!

He eagerly intercepted my lips with his. Strong arms wrapped around me, drawing me closer. A soft groan escaped Seth's lips as...

The screech of the dumpster lid yanked me out of the memory. Startled, I cowered closer to the shadow of the metal hulk. Someone dropped something inside the cavern, shut the lid with another echoing bang, and left with heels clicking against the pavement.

I shook, but not as much from the fear of being discovered as from the effects of the memory. That had been one of the few snapshots in the past year after Abby died when I was truly happy, if only for a brief moment.

Sobs choked me, but no sound came out. I couldn't breathe.

Seth had said he would love me in all times, but he wasn't even here in this time to love me.

I was suddenly, intensely angry. I picked up an empty, plastic water bottle beside me and threw it as hard as I could against the brick wall opposite. It made an unsatisfying little crackle at impact and fell harmlessly to the ground.

The shaking in my body had increased to near convulsions. Fear, rage, and grief mixed in a concoction that wouldn't release in tears.

So why wasn't I time traveling now? I had lost my grip on time after losing just Abby. Now that I had lost everyone, I stayed stuck in the same awful, distorted version of the future.

I knew the time hadn't changed. I'd been watching the same beer can across the alley since I'd sat down. It had stayed in that same position the entire time.

What good was the ability to time travel if I couldn't control or use it? I was stuck, and there was nothing I could do about it.

I took deep breaths of the garbage-laced air and tried to calm down. I wasn't afraid of time traveling. If fact, it would be a relief. I had never lost so much, and the intensity of emotion was overwhelming. What I didn't understand was why I was still here waiting to be apprehended by a powerful, evil Katherine and watching a stupid beer can in a disgusting alley.

Then it hit me.

There was no way I was going to relax enough to time travel back to where my biological body dictated I belonged. If I did, then I would land one day after Seth had shown up dead on the pier. I would be blamed for his murder, and worse than that, I would have to face life without him. Fear would ensure that I might not ever relax enough to time travel back to my own time.

The other way for me to time travel was if I experienced emotion so intense that it raised the levels of tempamine in my brain enough to make me slip into another time, which is what I kept expecting, and even wanting, to happen. But I just realized that wouldn't happen either—not because of fear, but because of hope.

I had controlled my time traveling once before. I had sent myself to a specific date in order to save Abby. Though I didn't know for sure how I had managed it, deep down there was a flicker of hope that I could control it again. Then I could save Seth, prevent Katherine from winning, rewrite the last ten years for Wayne, and make this future right.

That hope kept that beer can steady in my vision.

I didn't quite understand the full science of how my time traveling worked, but I somehow knew that the subconscious hope of changing things had kept me where I was, despite raging emotions. And it would continue to do so until it was fully extinguished or I figured out how to save my world.

I wasn't going to be suddenly whisked away to a

better time and place. I needed to figure out what to do now.

If I was a movie-worthy time traveler, then my future self would have already sent me some kind of message, telling me exactly how to get out of this mess. And yet here I waited, with possibilities on the horizon and no rescue in sight.

There was no one left to rescue me. The only people who knew about my time traveling were dead, except for Wayne. Well, there were other people who knew, but they were off-limits for me to contact. The first time I time traveled, I saved the Lawson family. I met them again five years later, which was actually only a few days later for me. They had believed my story, even the time traveling. However, when I time traveled to the future and found out the Lawsons were actually *my* family, I knew I couldn't maintain a relationship with them. I couldn't risk doing anything that might change the future of the Lawson's little baby girl growing up to become a scientist and, more importantly, my mother.

I dreamed of the day when my mother, Karis, would come and find me. I knew that after she sent her baby Hannah, me, back in the time machine, she would have to wait until things were safe before finding me. I knew that, at that point, I would be significantly older than my mother. But I also knew that it wouldn't matter. I would finally get to be a part of the Lawsons' family and have all secrets out in the open.

Until that day, I couldn't help but keep tabs on them. They had moved away from the Bay area for a few years while Matt finished his education to become a psychologist. After that, Matt got a job in the Bay area, and they moved back.

I had looked at their beautiful new house on Google Earth and checked out the website of Matt's employer. Seth teased that I cyber-stalked them, but somehow it helped to know the basics of where they were and what they were doing. I never made any contact, but I had their address and phone number memorized. That knowledge was the closest I would be able to get to my family for years. Even at this time, ten years later from when I was supposed to be, it would still be over twenty more years until I could safely contact them.

A crazy, twisted idea popped into my head.

Contacting some of the Lawsons didn't necessarily mean I had to interfere with Karis's life. Timmy and Maddie should be old enough to be on their own. I did some quick math. At this time, Maddie should be around twenty-six, and Timmy should be about twenty-three.

I sighed. It didn't really matter. I had no way to contact them. I had no access to a phone, no help, and no transportation. If there was some way for me to get a message to them, then I could ask them to pick me up.

I scoffed at the stupid thought. In order to get them a message, I would have had to send it sometime in the past. And now I was back at the drawing board—in an impossible situation that could be solved if I could just time travel!

Frustrated, I opened Seth's backpack and took out the notepad and pen from the hotel. With no hope and nothing else to do, I wrote the letter that would've saved me, had I sent it anytime in the past.

Dear Maddie and Tim,

The things people say about me aren't true. I am being framed.

Please meet me in the alley across from Deshaunds Art Gallery in San Francisco at the exact date and time listed below. I need a safe place to stay where I won't be found for an uncertain length of time. I also need food and a weapon to protect myself.

I am calling in a favor I earned on that snowy night when you two were children.

I need help now.

I took out my ferry ticket stub and copied the date. Trying to estimate the best I could, I also wrote the time.

Finally, I added one last line to the bottom:

P. S. I'm hiding behind the dumpster.

I didn't reread it. I didn't pause or let myself think about how pointless this all was. Instead, I quickly ripped the papers out of the notepad, folded, and slipped them inside a hotel envelope. In the center, I wrote Tim and Maddie's names, followed by the address I had memorized for their parents. I knew that there was the strong possibility that Matt and Kelly didn't live there anymore, but I was beyond dealing with the plausible. This was a fulfillment of the ridiculous because I had no other real hope to set my energy on.

In the corner for the return address, I thoughtfully wrote one word, 'Hannah.'

Finished, I held the envelope out and stared at it. If I ever managed to time travel to any point in the past, then I would buy a stamp and mail this letter. Then, just maybe, I could save myself and have a rescue waiting when facing this situation in some other timeline.

Tires screeched to a stop at the front of the alley. A car door slammed. Footsteps echoed on the cement, coming closer. I cowered, pressing myself against the cool, rusted metal of the dumpster and trying to blend in with the shadows.

A man appeared around the corner of the dumpster. He stopped and looked directly at me.

"Hannah, come on! Let's get out of here!"

My mouth fell open. I stared dumbly at the tall man and just sat there, curled in a ball against the dumpster. He was lean with sandy blond hair. He looked to be in his early twenties.

The side of his mouth quirked in a half-grin. He walked forward until he was right in front of me, then he squatted down so his face was near mine. Fun danced in his blue eyes.

"Hi, I'm Tim. I'm going to get you out of here."

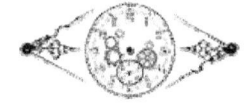

CHAPTER ELEVEN

AT his words, a memory surfaced of me leaning over a hurt little boy and saying that same thing: 'Hi, I'm Hannah. I'm going to get you out of here."

"T-Timmy?" I stuttered.

"Let's get you safe. Then we can talk," he said, seriousness returning as he helped me up.

He supported me as I limped toward the front of the alley where an SUV was parked.

I glanced down at the letter still clutched tightly in my hand. In shock and complete confusion, I glanced back in the alley, searching for that beer can. It lay in the exact same position.

I hadn't time traveled, yet Tim Lawson was here rescuing me as if in response to the letter I had just written.

Tim opened the door to the backseat and urged me in.

"Get down on the floor, Hannah," a gentle voice said from the front seat.

Maddie?

"You can't be seen," she explained.

I obediently ducked my head and slipped to the floor of the SUV. I struggled out of the backpack, but I continued to hold it close over my abdomen, as if it was a security blanket.

Tim got in the driver's side and pulled away from the alley. We drove for several minutes in complete silence. Tim was obviously concentrating on driving an intricate route. We turned so often, I lost track of all sense of direction. Feeling my left hand cramping, I looked back down at the envelope I still clutched. I carefully placed the letter in one of the backpack's exterior pockets and then zipped it completely closed.

I still didn't know what had happened. But at some point, I guess I had to mail the thing for sure now.

"Who knows about our connection to you, Hannah?" Tim finally asked from the front seat. "Who did you tell about saving our lives eighteen years ago?

"My parents, my sister, Seth, and Wayne were the only ones who ever knew," I replied, searching my memory to be sure. "The only one still alive is Wayne. He wouldn't even consider you guys as an option for me to go to. Besides, I really don't think he would reveal anything about me," I swallowed, "even under torture."

"We'll still need to be careful," Tim said. "Why wouldn't Wayne consider us an option? You obviously did."

"I was desperate," I replied quietly. "And I probably broke a dozen unwritten rules of time travel to do so. There are certain risks and facts that I can't really tell you. Besides, I only wrote the letter because I had no other option. I didn't think you'd actually receive it. And I take it, my letter was delivered at some point?"

"Yes," Maddie replied. "Though speaking of the rules of time travel, it probably wouldn't be a good idea for us to tell you when we received it. Things might work out differently from this point on. The point is, it came to Mom and Dad's house, and they gave it to us without opening it themselves."

"They must have a lot of trust in you," I said humbly.

"And you," Maddie said. "They knew it was from you, and you don't exactly have a stellar reputation, unless you consider infamy to be something to strive for. Yet they gave us the letter and never asked about it. I guess they figured if it was addressed to only Tim and I, then you must have had your reasons."

Tim pulled the vehicle over to the side of the road.

"Now's our chance," he said quickly. "I researched our route, and there are no cameras that cover about a twenty foot section right here. Hannah, crawl into the back right now. There is a large box back there. Put yourself in it and close the lid.

I refrained from asking questions and did exactly what Tim instructed. After folding myself and the backpack into the box and shutting the lid, I felt the SUV move again.

With my exhaustion and the movement of the vehicle, I think I dozed off at some point. I startled awake at the sound of a car door shutting. I heard the rear hatch open and felt myself being moved.

There was not a whisper of explanation before I felt myself being lifted in the box. I sat flat and hunched over, trying to keep my balance. After being set on the ground, the box tilted sideways, and I began to glide as if on wheels. I guessed that I was being moved with the aid of one of those dolly carts used to move appliances and other oversized items.

Sounds changed and became more dull-sounding, as if we had gone inside and were in a small, enclosed area. My stomach dropped as I felt sudden upward movement.

We were in an elevator. There were a few soft thuds and clanging of metal as the elevator stopped and we got out. A little more forward motion, a couple more turns, and I heard a door shutting, followed by the sound of locks being turned.

The lid came off the box, and I squinted in the sudden light.

"Sorry, Hannah," Tim said, his grinning face appearing over the top of the box. "We didn't want to chance anyone seeing you. I'm always bringing large equipment and boxes of supplies up here, so seeing me haul up another project isn't unusual."

Tim helped me out of the box.

I stretched my cramped muscles and looked around.

"Where are we?"

"This is home sweet home to Maddie and me," Tim replied. "We've been renting this flat for several months preparing for today. No one watching us should detect any unusual changes in our behavior. But you'll not be able to leave this apartment."

"Are we still in San Francisco?" I asked.

"Yes," Tim nodded. "We figured it's actually easier to stay hidden in a crowd."

Tim watched me as I limped around the flat. It was very large and open. I could see Maddie preparing food in the kitchen at one end. Some large windows fronted the flat, but they were all covered with either blinds or room-darkening curtains. A hallway in back of the kitchen probably led to the bedrooms, but this front room seemed to be a combination kitchen, living area, and workshop.

There was a couch, some chairs, and a TV in one corner, but the majority of the space was taken up with stuff that looked like it belonged in a garage. I wandered through different contraptions I couldn't identify and even some disgusting concoctions that looked like science experiments gone bad. There was an office space with several computers in one corner. Shelves lined the wall and were filled with books and equipment with no recognizable organization.

While standing near the office area, my gaze caught on something familiar. A miniature remote control car perched alone on a shelf. It was the same one I had given him the only other time I had seen the family after their accident.

I turned back to find Tim still watching me, a smile on his lips as he'd seen the direction of my gaze. It was somewhat disconcerting for me to realize that this was the same boy I had rescued. He and Maddie were now around my own age. Tim was taller than me and lean, yet well-muscled. There was not much of anything boyish left about him. Except his smile. When he smiled, he was that same little boy who had charmed me with his football-field length Christmas list of trucks.

"A San Francisco flat of this size has to cost a fortune!" I said, fighting twinges of guilt that they had already gone through so much time and expense to help me, someone they had really only met twice, if you count when I rescued them.

Tim shrugged casually. "There's a bakery downstairs. This flat takes up the entire second floor, and no one is above us. We needed something isolated. Price didn't really matter. Maddie is rich."

"You're not exactly hurting for money either, Tim!" Maddie shot back from the kitchen.

"What are you talking about?" Tim called back. "I'm still a poor student. You're the one who's loaded."

Even from a distance, I could see Maddie's eye roll.

"What do you do, Maddie?" I asked, crossing the room to sit on a barstool at the counter separating the kitchen from the rest of the room.

"Makeup," she replied simply, continuing to peel some carrots.

Tim let loose a loud guffaw. "Maddie saying she does makeup is like Mozart saying he does music!

At Maddie's lack of response, Tim explained. "Maddie has several chemistry degrees. She started her own makeup company with products that are organic and good for you. Saying she's been successful so far is putting it mildly. Fortunately, she has managed things so that she isn't the face of the company. Otherwise, we'd have some issues with staying under the radar."

I studied Maddie, remembering the thirteen-year old I'd given lip gloss to. She had returned from the restroom with a ridiculous amount of makeup caked on her face. Now that cute little face had grown into a beautiful woman. She was a light brunette with blue-gray eyes and the high cheekbones of a classic beauty. She was short and trim like her mom, though she seemed to lack her mom's outgoing personality. Instead of caked on makeup, her face now glowed with subtle highlights of makeup that looked natural yet enhanced her features.

"I'm pretty decent with chemistry myself," I said to Maddie. "I'm interested to hear more about what you do. Since Tim is so good at giving helpful information on you, how about you fill me in on what he does. I don't know that I can trust him. He says he's a student, but you seemed to indicate his income isn't too shabby either."

Maddie smiled shyly and put a platter of meats, breads, and assorted vegetables on the counter in front of me. Tim unceremoniously grabbed a plate and began assembling himself a huge sandwich.

Maddie swatted his hand away from the platter and handed me a plate. "Yes, you definitely can't trust Tim.

You never know when he's joking and when he's serious. But it's usually a good bet to figure he's joking 100 percent of the time."

I was so hungry. Needing no invitation, I began transferring food from the platter to my own plate

"Shall we pray first?" Maddie asked.

"Oh, come on Maddie!" Tim protested. "I'm starving! And Hannah probably hasn't eaten in days."

Maddie shot him a look that would make a saint squirm. She quickly bowed her head and prayed. "Dear, Lord, please bless this food to our bodies. Thank you for giving us the opportunity to help Hannah. Please give us wisdom to know how best to help her so that your purpose and will for her life prevails. In Jesus' name, Amen."

Tim immediately dug into his food, while I sat there staring at mine for several seconds. I hadn't thought there was anyone left to pray for me. I hadn't even been able to pray for myself.

Though Maddie's thoughtfulness and beautiful prayer touched me, it also brought back the familiar guilt. I wasn't on speaking terms with God because I hadn't trusted his purpose and will for my life. I thought I had screwed everything up beyond repair. I had thought there was no hope. But then Tim and Maddie had shown up.

"Tim is right," Maddie said, drawing me out of my thoughts. "He is a student. But he already has a couple of science degrees and is now working on his doctorate. He is an engineer of sorts and has already invented several useful gadgets, which explains his insistence on using our apartment as his own personal science lab. He has done some contracts with technology companies and has been quite successful himself."

I nodded. It sounded like a gift for science ran in the veins of my family, but I couldn't say that. Tim and Maddie didn't know that they were my biological uncle and aunt. And I had to make sure they didn't find out. I couldn't risk anything that may interfere with their sister, Karis, sending her baby back in time in a time machine.

"How are your parents?" I asked, trying to keep the conversation away from any serious topics.

"They're good," Maddie replied. At the moment, Tim had his mouth so full, he couldn't do more than grunt. "Dad has his own practice as a psychologist, and Mom works with me at my company. She handles the business side, while I handle the products."

"And your little sister?" I worked hard to keep my tone casual, as if it was just a polite inquiry.

Tim snorted. "Karis is a genius," he said around a mouthful of food. "She just turned 14 and is already whipping through college courses. She's interested in medicine. Mom and Dad call her Doogie Howser. I guess it's some guy off a TV show who was a kid doctor. I googled it once, but never made it through a full episode."

"It sounds like none of you are lacking in the brains department," I said.

Maddie shook her head. "Tim and I are smart, but Karis is different. They say she's some kind of prodigy."

Tim finished inhaling his food right as Maddie started assembling a sandwich for herself.

"Speaking of people with exceptional abilities, now it's your turn, Hannah." Tim pinned me with a direct gaze, leaving no room for me to escape to a different subject. I had been somewhat purposefully trying to guide the conversation away from myself. I knew I was in a gray area. I didn't know how much of my story I should reveal to Tim and Maddie. And if they asked too many questions, I didn't know how to keep our biological connection a secret.

"If we're going to help you, we need to know the full story," Maddie said. "Why are you here? You've obviously time traveled. The entire country is looking for a woman who should be a good ten years older than you appear."

"Maybe more importantly than that, we need to know how you time travel." Tim said with a face that was bright and eager. "Mom and Dad always thought you traveling back in time had been an isolated incident. They believed God had sent you specifically to save us. But apparently, it wasn't a one-time thing."

I could tell he had at least a thousand questions for me that had been stewing in his head for the past thirteen years.

I sighed. They were right. I needed their help, and there was no way around telling them as much as I could. I just had to be careful.

"My emotions cause me to time travel," I explained wearily. Feeling that every last cell in my body had expended all the energy it could, I limped over to the couch and sank down. "If I experience extreme emotion of any kind, then it can cause a neurotransmitter in my brain, tempamine, to spike, which induces time travel. When I am finally able to relax, the tempamine drops, allowing me to return to the time my body dictates is home. When I rescued your family, I was frightened of driving up that road to Silver Springs. Since then, just about every emotion has induced time travel at some point—anger, fear, even happiness."

Without pausing to allow them to voice the dozens of questions I could read on their faces, I skipped my other time traveling ventures and started with Abby's death, the event that had landed me in my current mess. I explained everything as quickly as I could, telling of my decision to go back and save my sister and then the resulting consequences. I also had to go back and fill in the details of Katherine's involvement with Jones-Stanton Pharmaceuticals and our efforts to stop them.

"So now I'm stuck. My family is dead. Seth is dead. Katherine is the governor of California. And I'm on the list for America's Most Wanted." Finishing, I looked at both Tim and Abby, desperate that they understand the jumbled mess and not run away from the catastrophe I'd created.

Tim looked thoughtful. "So we need to develop a plan to find a way to send you back to a time where you can fix this future."

I blinked, surprised. Seth and Wayne had always been reluctant about the idea of me purposely changing the future. Now Tim made the suggestion without hesitation.

"Yes, that's what I want to do. But I'm not sure how. Things get messy when I'm trying to go back and fix things and not run into myself."

"Yes, we'll have to develop a good plan and figure out an exact date to try to send you back to."

By the distant look in his eyes, I could tell Tim's mind was already off and scheming.

Maddie spoke up, "Hannah, I don't quite understand why you time travel. Tempamine isn't a normal brain chemical to have elevated. What causes you to react this way while others don't?

Drat! I was hoping to get by without that question!

As if sensing my hesitation, Maddie continued. "We just might be able to develop a better way to send you back in time, if we understood more of what triggered the time travel."

Taking a deep breath, I spoke quickly, yet carefully. "In one of my time traveling episodes, I found out that I was actually born in the future. I have subtle genetic abnormalities that made me a target for a genetic purity movement at the time. My parents sent me back in a time machine in order to save my life."

"A time machine!" Tim squeaked with eyes were as big as sand dollars. "Did you see it? What did it look like?"

"The genetic purity movement has already started," Maddie said calmly, seemingly unruffled by my explanation. "With nationalized insurance, there is a big push to only have children who will not put extra financial strain on the public."

"Traveling in the time machine was not without its consequences," I rushed to explain, hoping to deflate some of Tim's enthusiasm. "That's what caused the change in my brain chemistry, leading to my ability to time travel. Unfortunately, the time travel is also potentially deadly. Because of my genetic abnormalities, my body is able to handle tempamine levels that would normally kill someone, but after I return from a trip through time, the levels drop. I get side effects that worsen with each instance. Seth and Wayne developed some medication to save my life, but there is still concern that it will one day not be effective."

"So when you traveled to the future, what was it like?" Tim asked. "Did you see the time machine? Where did it come from?"

I really think his brain had stopped following my voice at the words 'time machine.'

I sighed. "Tim, there are some things I cannot tell you. I think I've already given you every detail I could, and probably a few I shouldn't have."

"Hannah is right," Maddie agreed, standing from where she had perched on a chair across from me. "The important thing now is that we keep her safe while we develop a plan to send her back in time to fix things."

"That reminds me," I said. "In my letter, I asked for some kind of weapon. You two aren't going to be able to stay around and babysit me all day. I'm sure you need to go to work, Maddie, and Tim has class. I need to be able to protect myself."

Brother and sister looked at each other.

"You can't exactly go out and buy a weapon in this day and age," Tim said hesitantly. "But we did sort of prepare for that as well. Or maybe I should say, Maddie prepared.

My gaze swung to Maddie as she took a classic karate stance.

"No problem, Hannah. I'll teach you to be your own weapon."

CHAPTER TWELVE

I lifted the curtain a tiny fraction and peered outside. Cars busied along the road and pedestrians hurried on their way, all blissfully unaware that I had been stuck in this same flat for a month.

I watched a woman in a red coat come out of the bakery below with a large box. I followed her with my eyes as she walked across the street and down the sidewalk, until she disappeared from view. I wanted to be that woman in the red coat. I wanted to have the freedom to buy food that wasn't good for me and then traipse down the sidewalk not caring who saw me. I wanted a purpose, a destination to go to in my red coat with my box of goodies.

I sighed. Instead, I was stuck. Today was the same as every other day this past month. I was trapped and left to only dream of freedom, a red coat, and a box of fresh confections.

The delicious smells of donuts and pastries wafting

up from the bakery below only added to the torture. I hoped Tim would at least bring me up some of the leftover bakery goods when he came home tonight. The owner frequently let him have his pick at the end of the day for little or no cost.

And then I hoped my unsettled stomach would allow me to eat them. I had been so stressed lately that my digestive system was in constant knots.

Tim, Maddie, and I had spent the entire month developing plan after plan that never made it past the idea stage. Every inspiration had a fatal flaw. There didn't seem to be any way to go back in time and change things without encountering myself or running the risk of making things worse.

There was so much we didn't know. We didn't know what had happened to Mr. Smith. If I went back in time and preemptively managed to get the evidence against Katherine and Jones-Stanton, I had no way of contacting Mr. Smith to arrange an earlier hand-off.

Our current, best idea was to forget the potential of the universe falling in on itself and go back in time to simply warn the other Seth and Hannah. Unfortunately, there was no guarantee that it would work. If I prevented them from going to Fort Baker Pier, Seth would have to reconnect with Mr. Smith somewhere, and there was just as great a potential that he would be killed at a later rendezvous.

I sighed. I couldn't stay here forever. Tim and Maddie were gone all day, which was good. They had been able to maintain their schedules and no one was the wiser that they had a new roommate. The search for me on the outside was still fierce. But the effects of staying in a dark flat for a solid month with nothing to do were starting to increase my already challenging depression and desperation.

A loud bang sounded from behind me.

I jumped at least six inches off the floor and turned mid-air.

Three feet in front of me stood someone dressed in the long, black, hooded costume of death.

I let out a strangled screech and took off.

About ten steps into my sprint, I suddenly stopped. The image I had seen caught up with the sudden shock of terror. Death was holding a frying pan and a metal spoon. And he was wearing a pair of very familiar blue tennis shoes.

"Timmy!" I shrieked. "You jerk!"

Picking up cards and magazines off the floor and pillows from the couch, I began flinging everything at him as fast as I could.

Death cowered, putting his hands over his face as chuckles of laughter escaped.

"Alright! Stop!" he called. "I give! You win!"

Tim straightened and pulled the black hood off his head. I sent one last pillow sailing straight into his face.

"Well, that didn't work as I'd hoped," he said, tossing the offending pillow to the floor and grinning from ear to ear.

"What were you trying to do? Give me a heart attack?"

"No! I was trying to scare you into a different time!"

"With a frying pan?" I threw back, still very angry.

"The frying pan was just to make a loud noise." Tim defended. "You were supposed to be gone before you realized it was a frying pan and me."

"What a horrible plan! I told you before that the only way I time traveled back on purpose before was that I was focused on a certain date, the day before Abby died. You had no idea of what I was thinking. I could have been thinking about dinosaurs, and you could have sent me back in time to be eaten by a T Rex!"

"Now that would be totally cool!"

I launched another pillow at his enthusiastic grin.

"Seriously, Tim, don't ever do that again," I said in my best grown-up voice. Tim was technically only a year younger than me at this point. But he still reminded me so often of that little boy that I didn't know that I would ever think of him any differently. I very consciously worked to think of him as 'Tim,' but to me, he'd always be 'Timmy.'

I explained seriously, "If we are going to try the plan where I go back to warn the other Seth and Hannah, then we need a good plan that lets me focus on that specific date.

"I disagree," Tim said, pulling the death costume off and tossing it on the floor. He flopped on the couch. "From what you told me, I think the only reason you were able to time travel back to save Abby was that Seth did something so unexpected, it scared you to death. If you know what's coming, you won't experience the extreme emotion of the unknown."

"That's what Seth said," I grumbled, flopping on the couch beside Tim. "So what are we going to do?"

"I'm working on it," he said thoughtfully. "I'll let you know when I come up with something brilliant. Or maybe I won't let you know."

"Tim," I said, warning in my voice. "Wait a minute! What are you doing home now anyway? I thought you were going to be late with a class."

"The class was cancelled," he supplied, leaning his head back in a relaxed position and propping his feet on the coffee table. "So I guess it's just you and me for dinner. What are you making?"

I swatted his arm playfully. With nothing else to do with my imprisonment, I usually made dinner for all of us. But I'd learned that Tim was a relentless tease and never missed an opportunity to teasingly take me for granted or comment on my rather unique culinary skills.

"Where's Maddie?" I asked. "Isn't she going to be home for dinner?"

"No. She's out with her boyfriend. She said she'd be back late."

I nodded. From what I could tell, Maddie had a fairly serious boyfriend. Part of me wondered though if she would be even more serious about him if I wasn't around. She only went out with him about once a week, and it would probably be more if the sweet woman wasn't bent on doing whatever she could to help and keep me entertained.

"Do you not have a girlfriend, Tim?" I asked, realizing that Tim was home every night. He never seemed to go out socially.

"Oh, sure!" he replied. "I have several."

I rolled my eyes. "I somehow have no doubt that you do!" The fun was short-lived, however, as I turned serious. "I do feel bad, Tim. I feel like you and Maddie are risking your lives and putting them on hold to help me. If I wasn't around, Maddie would go out more, and you could spend more time entertaining those girlfriends."

Tim scoffed. "Hannah, this past month has been a blast for me, even though you can't really cook and you won't give me any details on that time machine… at all. And don't feel bad about Maddie. I don't like her boyfriend that much anyway. He's nowhere near good enough for her. And he has the most annoying laugh."

Maddie was the sweetest person I'd ever met. She was calm, genuine, and had a very sincere faith. She was good for me to be around, kind of an anchor in the hurricane swirling around me. If I ever managed to fix things and get back to my own time, she would be the one thing I would miss from this time. Of course, I'd miss Tim as well, but Maddie had very quickly become a forever friend. In my time, she was a sixteen-year-old girl, and I couldn't be a part of her life. Whereas I had trouble seeing Tim as an adult, I had no trouble at all seeing Maddie as a respected peer. I didn't like to think of a day when I couldn't have her friendship.

"Tim, there's no guy on the planet who would be good enough for Maddie," I said genuinely.

"True," Tim agreed. "But she could at least find someone who didn't laugh like a machine gun singing soprano."

I shook my head. I wasn't going to let Tim sidetrack the conversation with his ridiculous comments. Maddie's boyfriend aside, I still feel bad. I'm putting you both in danger that I never intended. I appreciate you coming to my rescue, but I still don't understand how it happened. I wrote the letter, but I never sent it, at least I haven't sent it yet. But you received it, and now I'm doing a great job of ruining your lives."

"First of all, you aren't ruining our lives at all." Tim said, putting his arm on the back of the couch so he could face me more directly. For once, all teasing had left his eyes, and he was serious. "We wouldn't even be alive if you hadn't saved us eighteen years ago. As far as the letter, I have a theory. Has there ever been another time when an instant decision caused an immediate result, even though it hadn't technically happened yet?"

"You already know the answer to that," I said wearily.

Tim had spent the last month grilling me on the details of every time traveling experience I'd had. I worked to keep back any information that may prove dangerous, but it was difficult. Thankfully, he still didn't know about my connection to his sister as I flat-out refused to tell him anything about my trip to the future.

Tim seemed to be waiting patiently for me to continue.

I threw my hands up in exasperation. "I already told you about how I was stuck with Wayne for a month after Abby died. You know how I had to call myself to get my art supplies so I could try to relax and travel forward a year. Right when the other Hannah said she would bring my kit, I had a memory of placing it at Wayne's door, even though it technically hadn't happened yet."

Tim leaned forward. "In both cases, you saw the result before the cause actually happened. With your art kit, you had the memory before the kit was actually delivered. With your letter, you experienced the effects of the letter before you actually sent it. Don't you see what the two instances have in common, Hannah?"

"No," I said, staring at him blankly.

"You! With the art kit, the instant the other Hannah made the decision, you had the memory because the decision is what caused the action. It was a foregone conclusion at that point that the art kit would be the delivered. There were no potential factors that could interfere. The cause of the memory wasn't the actual action; it was the decision that led to the action."

"Okay," I said slowly, struggling to follow his logic. "So you're saying that, in the absence of interference, the decision to act is what produces the result, not necessarily the action itself."

"Correct," Tim replied happily.

"But that can't be the same case with the letter. Yes, I wrote the letter and made the decision to mail it if I should ever travel back in time again, but I have to have an interfering factor in order to time travel! Unlike the other situation, it isn't solely dependent on my will!"

"That's where you're wrong, Hannah. After all this time, I don't think you understand your time traveling at all. It *is* dependent on you. You are the only factor that produces the result. Whether you embrace it or not is the question, but I don't think there is any question of whether you can control it. You already do. Yes, you let other factors influence you. You lose control of your emotions, but you are the one who dictates when and where you travel. That should be obvious in that you were able to travel back to a specific date to save Abby."

"You think that my decision to mail the letter from the past ensured it would happen because I am the only variable when it comes to my time travel?"

"Correct. Your decision ensured the future action. Whether you learn to control your time traveling now or ten years from now, I think at some point you will. If you face enough motivation, whether that motivation is internal from your desire or external from events causing you intense emotion, you time travel. The challenge for you will be to switch your time travel from being caused by external stimulus to an internal stimulus. In other words, you have to figure out how to do it when you want to and not when you don't."

"It's a lovely theory, Tim. But I think you're wrong. My time traveling has plagued me since day one. It's almost killed me numerous times, and now it has ruined my life and cost me nearly everyone I love. If it was possible for me to control, don't you think I would have figured it out by now. If desire to time travel had anything to do with it, I wouldn't have stayed in this time for a single hour."

"You're misunderstanding me, Hannah. I'm not saying that any of this is your fault or that any amount of desire on your part would cause you to time travel. Instead, I want you to be encouraged. This isn't going to last forever. You will time travel again, and I believe you will have the chance to fix things. In my mind, it's a biological certainty."

"Thank you, Timmy," I said, feeling weak as the frustration and anger left at his soft-spoken answer. "With you handling the science end and Maddie praying and handling the faith side of things, I should be covered, right?"

Then why did I feel so lost and hopeless?

"What do you want to eat for dinner?" I stood and walked quickly toward the kitchen. I needed a change of subject and a task to keep my mind occupied. "Oh, wait a minute, maybe you should cook, Tim. Didn't you say just a while ago that I can't cook?"

"I didn't really mean that you're a bad cook…" Tim hedged, looking wary at the threat of having to do his own cooking.

"I'm just not especially good?"

Whereas my cooking might not be gourmet, his was inedible. He tried to surprise Maddie and me with breakfast one morning. We had been thoroughly impressed that he had managed to burn the eggs while still keeping them runny.

Tim hesitated. "Well, your tacos aren't bad."

"But are they good?

Tim brightened. "We have that big jar of salsa, right?"

I smirked. "You can have whatever is left after I dump it over your head, okay?"

Not looking scared in the least, Tim grinned and flopped back on the couch while I began pulling out the ingredients for tacos.

Seth hadn't ever complained about my cooking. I knew I wasn't the best. Abby had confiscated all of our Grandma's skill in the culinary arts. I could follow a recipe though. The best I could figure, Tim's problem was that he was spoiled. I had a feeling that his mom, Kelly, was a fabulous cook.

At least Maddie never complained. Admittedly, Maddie was a Pollyanna. Sometimes, there seemed more of a chance of the sun deciding not to come up than of Maddie saying one unkind word.

I made quick work of preparing the tacos, and Tim and I ate with light, companionable banter. Thankfully, he didn't again broach the subject of time travel. Though I knew he would probably love to discuss Plan Z or grill me on some vague detail in one of my trips through time, he probably realized that I was at my limit for the day.

After Tim helped with the dishes, I retired to my room and left him to work on his projects.

A couple of hours later, I was still wide awake and trying to make it through yet another time travel romance on the Kindle Maddie had lent me. With nothing else to do, I had started reading every fiction time travel book I could find. Mostly I wanted a little distraction and entertainment, but I deliberately chose time travel because I was also hoping for a little inspiration.

With my ears already on high alert, I heard the front door of the flat open, and I eagerly hopped off my bed. Maddie was home!

Not caring that I was in pink pajamas and slippers, I met her as she was hanging up her purse right inside the door.

"Did you have a good time?" I whispered eagerly. Maddie was my window to the outside world. Thankfully, she didn't seem to have a problem with me living vicariously through her.

"Yes, we had a nice evening," she whispered back calmly, casting a glance Tim's direction.

Tim hadn't acknowledged her arrival, and we didn't expect him to. The only time Tim was serious for longer than about five minutes was when he was working on one of his projects. Then he was so focused he didn't like to be disturbed. Since he usually liked to work after dinner and late into the night, Maddie and I usually snuck off to talk or watch TV together in one of our rooms.

"I'm sorry I'm so late," Maddie said worriedly. "Did you still want to practice? I think you're almost done with that kata."

"No, that's okay," I assured her. "We can skip it

tonight. I practiced earlier."

Maddie had been faithfully teaching me self-defense for the past month. Though I had my doubts about my skills, Maddie was an excellent teacher and was pleased with my progress. After teaching me basic self-defense techniques, she had progressed to teaching me some more formal katas.

"I'd rather hear all about your date with Evan," I said, raising my eyebrows at her expectantly. "Besides, we don't want to wake the dragon."

Tim wasn't exactly mean if we disturbed him, but both Maddie and I hated the pointed, annoyed glares and the loud tossing of his supplies if we should disturb him.

Maddie nodded. "Let's grab some M&Ms and head to my room. I could use some chocolate. Dinner was pretty fancy, which I guess means a big price for little food."

I nodded and readily headed for our chocolate stash in the cupboard.

Maddie followed behind me. She sat on a barstool and slipped off her shoes as I reached to get the M&M's that had been shoved behind a set of salad bowls in hope that Tim wouldn't find them.

"Hannah, are you sure no one can connect you to us?" Maddie said thoughtfully from her perch.

Startled by her unexpected question, I yanked the M&M sack too hard, causing the salad bowls to clang together loudly. I turned, noting Maddie's pensive and slightly troubled expression. I quickly opened the sack, popped a few candies in my mouth, and offered it to

Maddie.

She took a pitiful few and returned it to me. Taking the rest of her share along with my own second serving, I tried to calm my sudden anxiety with large amounts of chocolate.

Maddie's question was a little disconcerting, but the look on her face unnerved me.

"Yes, I'm sure," I said, trying to be more casual and confident than I felt. No one outside of my family and Wayne knew, and like I said before, Wayne would never make the connection that I would go to you for help. He wouldn't view it as an option."

Seeing that Maddie's face still looked troubled, I stuffed a few more M&M's in my mouth. "Why do you ask, Maddie? Did something happen?"

Maddie shrugged and said quietly, "I thought I saw a boy with a helium balloon today."

My stomach dropped like the M&M's had been lead weights. Helium was not a good thing.

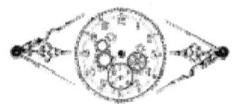

CHAPTER THIRTEEN

"HELIUM?" Tim's voice shot from the other side of the room. "Maddie, did you say helium?

I had difficulty swallowing the last M&M I'd shoved in my mouth.

Tim, Maddie, and I had developed a code word system based on the periodic table. It was mostly for Tim and Maddie's use. They could call each other and casually mention one of the code words, and the other person would immediately know what was going on. Tim had given me an untraceable burner phone in case either one of them needed to contact me in an emergency. But so far, I had never received a call on my phone, and we have never had to use the code words.

If lithium was mentioned, that meant that something relevant to me had happened in the news. Carbon meant someone had asked suspicious questions. Oxygen meant the entire situation was compromised and there was immediate danger. Neon meant you had been apprehended.

There were a few other bizarre ones that Tom had come up with, but I had trouble remembering all of them. It had actually been hilarious coming up with the code and brainstorming different ways to insert the elements in casual conversation. Lithium batteries, carbonated soda, carbon dioxide, neon signs, a Dodge Neon car—our list had been exhaustive in every way.

Now at the mere whispered mention of helium from across the room, Tim abandoned his project and was at our side in seconds, cornering Maddie with an intense interrogation.

"Helium, Maddie?" he asked grimly. "Are you sure?"

"No, I'm not sure," she replied, clearly uncomfortable with Tim's intensity. "I couldn't identify anyone suspicious, but at several points today, I definitely felt like I was being followed."

"Did you see anyone?" Tim asked.

Maddie sat on a barstool and wearily answered. "At lunch, I saw two men in suits across the restaurant. They kept looking my direction, but I can't be sure they were watching me. For the most part, I just kept getting goose bumps all day like I was being watched."

"Well, that doesn't sound too bad," I said with a tad too much optimism. "Maybe the suit guys were just checking you out."

"Did you take precautions?" Tim asked, ignoring my comment.

"Of course." Maddie nodded. "That's why I'm so

late. I didn't let Evan bring me home, but took a taxi and two buses for the long way home. I'm not sure why I bothered. I know we route everything through a post office box, but it wouldn't take much to find out where I lived."

Tim leaned against the counter. Unlike Maddie, his face didn't look worried, scared, or even stressed. He was just thoughtful. "You're right. If they really are suspicious, then they could come search our flat here at any time."

"Hannah says she can't be traced to us." Maddie sat up straight and seemed to purposely force her thoughts in a different direction. "I'm probably being paranoid. Like I said, I didn't really see anyone."

Tim and I nodded, though in my heart, I realized the chances of Maddie being wrong were slim. Maddie was observant and intuitive. If she thought she was being followed, she probably was.

"I probably shouldn't have even mentioned it." Maddie continued, now backpedaling faster as she worked to erase the stress from her features. "It wasn't anything conclusive. I'm sorry guys; I likely put you through a helium false alarm."

"No, Maddie, don't feel bad," Tim assured. "You did the right thing. We need to be aware of any potential threat, real or imagined."

Despite his words, the look on Tim's face said he didn't buy her paranoid excuse either.

"Are you clear on the plan," he asked, turning to me.

"Yes," I said hesitantly, not liking the sudden change in subject. "But I still don't like that last part."

"Don't worry about it," Tim said easily. "That's only the last resort. Plan Z."

"I still don't like the idea of jumping out a window. Not to mention that Geno the baker won't be happy about me ruining his awning."

Tim shrugged, "You'll be fine. It's a soft landing. And Geno has been looking for an excuse to replace that awning anyway. But, with any luck, you'll time travel well before you get to that point anyway. Bad guys show up, you'll freak out, and it's bye bye Hannah."

"With my luck, I'll jump, miss, and break multiple bones," I muttered.

"Better to have a few broken bones than the alternative of being captured and facing Katherine Colson and certain death."

"True," I admitted, shoving a few more M&Ms in my mouth. I had been steadily grazing since Maddie mentioned helium. "But certain death isn't really the part that concerns me."

I got chills just thinking about Katherine and what she had possibly put my family through. I had told Tim and Maddie everything I had learned from Wayne. Even though I would have rather left the terrifying parts out, I knew they needed to have a full picture of what we were up against and the risks I was exposing them to.

"As exhilarating as this conversation is, I'm going to bed," Maddie interrupted wearily. Though she had successfully eased some of the worry from her countenance, she was still clearly exhausted. "I'm sorry, Hannah, I'm not up to a chat session tonight after all. It's been a long day, and I have to wake up and go into the office early again tomorrow."

As Maddie stood from her stool, I moved to hand her more M&Ms. After the few token candies she had taken when I first offered the sack to her, I suddenly realized I'd forgotten to share.

Maddie now accepted the bag and looked inside. Smiling, she handed the bag back to me. "That's okay, Hannah. The last M&M is yours."

Embarrassed, I looked in the bag and saw it was empty except for one green candy nestled in the corner. "I'm sorry, Maddie! I didn't mean to hog them all."

"Don't feel bad. I swiped the other bag on my way to work this morning." Maddie moved toward the hallway and her room. "Goodnight!"

Sighing, I tossed the empty candy bag in the trash. "I guess I'll head to bed too and let you get back to work, Tim." Unfortunately, I had a feeling that 'heading to bed' meant I would lie down and run lists through my head, trying to keep my thoughts from straying to stress and grief. There was almost no chance of sleep, especially after the helium scare. Chances were good that instead, I would recite the books of the Bible, the periodic table of elements, the Gettysburg address, all the states and capitals, several sonnets, and as many Bible verses as I could remember while sleep taunted me.

Tim didn't respond to my goodnight announcement. I

saw that he was staring off into space, obviously deep in thought. It looked like he was already turning back into serious, night-time Tim.

I knew it would be pointless to try to interrupt his extreme focus, so I left him to his thoughts and headed down the hall to my room.

"You know you look ridiculous," Tim called after me.

I turned to look at him.

He nodded toward the backpack perched on my back.

I looked down at my pink pajamas borrowed from Maddie. I guess I probably did look ridiculous wearing Seth's backpack with my pajamas, but I had not let the backpack leave my person in the entire month I'd been here. I wasn't going to start now. I lived minute to minute, never knowing if or when I would time travel or be apprehended. That backpack held the medicine that would save my life if I ever did go back to my own time.

I reached up and idly fingered the locket around my neck. It was the other item that never left my body. For despite everything that happened, the backpack and locket still symbolized a hope that I would time travel again and have the chance to fix what had gone wrong.

I looked at Tim and shrugged. "Better safe than sorry. And with the possibility of helium…"

Tim nodded. "I guess it would be comforting, so you don't have to sleep alone, though I can't imagine a backpack would be a cozy bedfellow." Though the tone of the comment was serious, I saw his eyes dancing.

I made a face at him and turned back to my room.

Tim never missed an opportunity to tease me. And the ever-present backpack gave him ample ammunition. As ridiculous as it may seem, I wore the thing everywhere—when I ate, used the bathroom, and slept. I couldn't risk not having it with me when I time traveled.

Halfway through listing famous artists in order of their birth, I started to drift off to sleep. My mind drifted back to the night I first time traveled and saved the Lawsons. That same night is what brought Seth into my life. His blond hair and blue-green eyes swam through my memory.

I suddenly sat straight up in bed.

I'd been wrong. Seth, Wayne, and my family weren't the only ones who knew about that night. With very little research, that person would have been able to connect me to the Lawsons.

Ice flowed through my veins.

Someone did know. And that someone was the one person who filled me with terror.

CHAPTER FOURTEEN

I awoke to an awful smell—a *really* awful smell. It smelled like coffee, but it was sour, almost like gym shoes.

I crawled off my bed, adjusted the backpack, and went to investigate. Tim must be home. He had left for class this morning, before I'd gotten up. Though it was a Saturday, Maddie was gone too, probably to her office. I had gotten dressed, but then, bored out of my mind, I'd gone back to bed and tried to catch up on the pitiful little sleep I'd had last night.

The smell got more intense the closer I got to the kitchen / living room area.

"What is that disgusting smell?" I threw out the question as I entered the large room, practically gagging.

Tim looked up from where he was seated by his computer, blinking in surprise. "Oh, it's just an experiment."

"Well, I think the experiment is a failure and should never again be attempted! You're going to need toxic waste disposal for that stuff!"

"Come on, it's not that bad. It's just coffee."

He didn't seem to realize how bad it actually was. The coffee must have cauterized his sense of smell.

I scowled. "Coffee doesn't smell like gym shoes."

Tim cocked a grin and walked over to check the pot. "Well, apparently *yours* does! I found the package on the counter. I think you left it there yesterday when you were reorganizing your backpack for the fiftieth time. You don't drink coffee, so I figured you wouldn't mind if I used it for a project."

Reorganizing the backpack was an obsessive compulsion for me. I had gradually removed some things and added others, turning the backpack into the ultimate survival kit. Yesterday, I finally decided to part with the coffee and some of the other complimentary items I had taken from the hotel room. I should have known that Tim would recycle the things I'd discarded. Most trash in the flat got adopted into one of Tim's projects at some point.

After swirling the coffee around in examination, Tim put the pot back on the heat. I groaned. I was apparently in for the long haul with the coffee experiment.

I swallowed and tried to ignore my nausea. If the coffee was going to be poisoning the room indefinitely, my stomach might revolt and breakfast might make a return trip.

Of course, the sick feeling in the pit of my stomach

could also have been caused from a sudden case of anxiety. Bad coffee or not, I needed to talk to Tim.

I spoke in a rush, wanting to get it out before I lost my nerves. "Tim, I was wrong. There is someone else who might be able to connect me to you and Maddie. I remembered last night. After I saved your family that night eighteen years ago, I disappeared back to my own time. Seth searched for me. He told his friends about the story of me rescuing your family. I'm sure Katherine heard it. Though your names were never mentioned to her, it might not matter. If she remembers how Seth and I originally met, then she can probably trace back the event of your accident and find your names. It doesn't seem likely that she would remember and make the connection, but there is a possibility."

Tim's eyebrows rose in interest, but he didn't seem disturbed. "I know that's unsettling for you, Hannah, but I've always known this wasn't a long-term solution. Whether Katherine connects the dots or someone else does, you're going to be discovered. Staying in this flat with the curtains drawn is not a five-year plan."

I knew he was right, but I couldn't stop the reflexive shudder that rippled through my body.

Seeing my reaction, Tim put his arm around my shoulder in a gentle squeeze. "Don't worry about it, Hannah. That's why we have the plan. Maddie's supposed to be home by noon today, which should be any time. When she gets here, we'll have some lunch and talk about a plan to get you to time travel so you can fix everything."

I nodded and tried to tell myself that I was really in

no more danger than yesterday. Nothing had changed. I just now realized anew how fragile my refuge was.

"I know!" Tim said with sudden enthusiasm. "How about a cup of coffee to soothe your nerves?"

I shrugged out of his one-armed embrace and swatted him playfully. "Drinking your disgusting concoction would probably launch me a few decades! No thank you!"

Tim's eyes lit up with inspiration. "Now there's an idea! Maybe we could chemically induce your time travel! Eating something you hate or giving you a mild stimulant might—"

Two loud thumps sounded from the door, cutting Tim off.

"Let me go!" Someone screamed.

My heart leapt into my throat. It was Maddie's voice.

"I can't breathe!" She shrieked. "Oxygen! I need oxygen!"

"Hannah, the plan!" Tim hissed.

I sprang toward the hallway. Out of the corner of my eye, I saw Tim run to the wall and hit a switch. Hopefully his part of the plan would buy me enough time to accomplish mine.

The thumps on the door continued, beating a cadence to Maddie's screams. It sounded like she was kicking the door while someone else was working at the lock.

Tremors shook the whole length of my body, and fear

constricted my throat.

This was what we had prepared for. This was the day my worst fears came true. Yet there was also a sense of unreality about it, as if I was watching the scene play out in a movie.

I opened the closet by the bathroom, pushed aside the coats, and pulled up the door to the old, broken dumbwaiter.

The plan was for me to hide inside until the danger was past. We had rigged a bottom in the old shaft and stocked the small space with food and water. I could just fit myself inside. Then I would put a lid on top of my hiding space. If someone inspected the dumbwaiter, it would look like it was broken and had been blocked off years ago.

I hoisted my leg up to crawl inside.

A pair of hands grabbed either side of my arms and pulled me back.

I screamed and hit the floor.

I was pulled roughly to my feet.

Gaining my balance, I reacted automatically. I drew my foot back and slammed it as hard as I could into the person behind me. I felt something give on impact. My attacker yelped in pain and automatically relaxed his hold. I swung around. Raising my leg, I kneed him in the crotch at the same time I drove the palm of my hand into his nose, forcing his head back. Shrieks of agony echoed through the flat as he crumpled to the ground.

I ran, not stopping to think about the pain I had

caused him. I hadn't thought about what to do; my body had just responded with an almost animal-like instinct for escape. The end result being that I had done everything Maddie had taught me. I hadn't fought fair. I had hit him where he was most vulnerable and done what I needed to do to live.

I headed down the hallway to the back of the flat, knowing I now needed to use the back-up plan of the fire escape. A large man appeared directly between me and the exit. I slid to a stop, and we stood, frozen and staring at each other for the briefest of seconds.

The other man who had attacked me must have come up the fire escape as well. There was no way they could have made it through Timmy's obstacle course that quickly.

I spun and ran back down the hall. I heard the man behind me grunt and his footsteps thud against the hardwood of the hallway. I rounded the corner into the kitchen.

The room was in chaos. I glimpsed Maddie at the open front door. She was screaming and kicking as a woman and two men were trying to hold her down. Tim was by his computer, orchestrating the chaos in between him and Maddie. He had set up a complicated system of traps and obstacles, which looked as if it was working beautifully. Several men already lay groaning on the floor. One man took off in a sprint toward Tim, right as a frying pan flew from the ceiling on a wire and knocked him directly in the face.

I dodged around a man who had made it to the kitchen. I swerved toward the refrigerator, but his hand gripped my backpack. I twisted. His grip held fast, pulling me back.

Desperate, I reached out to the counter. My fingers latched onto the handle of the coffee pot containing Tim's experiment. I shrugged one arm out of my backpack and spun around to my assailant. Without pause, I took off the lid and threw the hot coffee. It hit him in the chest and splashed down his front. He released me, yelling curses as he screeched in pain.

I ran to the window, my backpack flopping against my back. I threw back the curtains and slid open the glass. I hoisted myself on the window sill and tried to breathe.

Plan Z.

If all else failed, if all other escape routes were blocked, I was supposed to jump out the window and land on the blue and white striped awning of the bakery below

I swallowed and looked down.

All of the air in my lungs suddenly froze, and I couldn't breathe.

There was no awning.

Bare spines awaited below, no longer supporting the canvas of the bakery's awning. Geno must have found the excuse he needed to replace the old awning. It was a possibility we'd never considered.

There was no backup for Plan Z.

Terrified, I looked back over my shoulder, desperately searching for another option.

The invaders were getting the upper hand. One of the

men had reached Tim. With Tim's hand wrenched behind his back, the man was pulling him away from the computer as Tim struggled to free himself.

My gaze collided with Tim's, and he suddenly stopped struggling.

"Jump, Hannah!" he yelled.

I started to protest. I wanted to yell back that the awning was gone. But at the look on Tim's face, I realized he already knew. Tim made a daily habit of checking every element in the plan. The dumbwaiter was checked every morning along with all of his equipment. He even checked the window by sliding it open and closed and looking out to scout out the landing.

He knew that the awning was gone. Yet he was still ordering me to jump.

I glanced back. We were on the second floor. I would get injured and possibly die.

I looked back at Tim, shaking my head. I couldn't do it.

The man I'd thrown the coffee at stood up from the kitchen floor. Growling in fury, he lunged toward me and the window with murder on his face.

"Do it now, Hannah!" Tim ordered, his shout firm and commanding. "Jump!

Turning back around, I took one last look at the pavement below and leapt out the window.

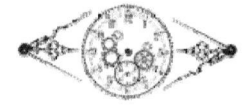

CHAPTER FIFTEEN

I felt the coffee man's fingertips brush my arm as gravity pulled me out of his reach. I closed my eyes tightly, the air rushing past me in two seconds of free fall. I braced myself, waiting for the impact of concrete. My feet hit something soft that gave beneath me, slowing my fall but toppling me backwards. My eyes flew open at a sickening cracking sound. My arms flailed as I was wrapped in some kind of hard material. Before it registered that I was falling again, I was sliding, and my back hit the ground.

The air was knocked out of me. My chest felt paralyzed, and I couldn't inhale. I lay still, blinking up to see the remaining spines of the awning with the blue sky beyond.

I heard shouting. Struggling to a sitting position, I found myself wrapped in blue and white striped canvas.

The awning that hadn't been there seconds before

was now wrapped around my legs.

I drew in air and struggled to my feet, fighting the canvas and the pain in my back. A few people gathered around, staring at me with open mouths, yet not one of them offered to help or asked if I was okay.

The shouting got louder and the front door to the bakery opened. A very large, angry man with flailing arms rushed toward me. I took off. I pushed past the bystanders and ran down the sidewalk. I heard Geno the baker behind me, but by the time I reached the corner, he was huffing and puffing a good distance behind me.

I turned right. Seeing an alley across the street, I sprinted across two lanes of traffic, barely missing a taxi turning the corner behind me. I shot into the alley. After several more turns behind buildings, I stopped and dropped to the ground in the shadowy corner of a brick building. I leaned my head against my upright knees and tried to catch my breath.

My heart rate slowed, and the panic receded. They hadn't caught me. This wasn't like the last time I had to hide out in an alley. I had a plan.

I knew I had time traveled. That was the only explanation for how the awning had suddenly appeared to break my fall.

Timmy would love that I had time traveled mid-air! As terrifying as it had been, he had been right.

I rummaged in my backpack and pulled out a stocking cap and some sunglasses. This time I'd opted for the simplest disguise possible, not wanting to take up precious cargo space in the backpack. I stuffed my hair in the cap, slid on the sunglasses, and stood, making my way to where the alley exited to a main road.

Now I just had to figure out *when* I was.

I cautiously looked out. Not seeing anything suspicious, I took a deep breath and exited the alley. Careful not to make eye contact with any other pedestrians, I walked down the sidewalk to the nearest corner. I checked the names of the streets, recognizing immediately where I was. All of those hours I'd spent the past month pouring over maps of San Francisco had paid off. I walked one more block and stood at a lamppost, watching the electronic ticker tape of a large sign on a bank. The date flashed by.

December 22. I'd traveled back only six months from my previous time.

I took a deep breath and tried to not suffocate under the sudden shroud of discouragement. I was hoping to land sometime before Seth had died. Now I'd time traveled and still didn't have a chance to fix things. I'd needed something before December 19th, when Seth had died, and definitely a date more than 10 years before now. December 22nd did me no good. I hadn't even managed to get the day of the month right.

I continued walking down the sidewalk, trying to tell myself that this could still work. The important thing was that I was safe, at least for the moment. I could have another chance to time travel and change things. Right now, nobody in this time knew of my presence. All hope was not lost.

I had a plan.

Tim, Maddie, and I had never discussed what I would do after I time traveled, whether that be to my target time or not. Other than floating out ideas of how I could change history, I hadn't mentioned where I would go or how I would keep from being discovered. I kept it to myself because I didn't want them to ever be put in the position of being forced to reveal what they knew about my plans. Discretion was a matter of safety, both for me, and for them.

I zigzagged through a combination of streets and alleys, following a route along the map in my head.

A few days after I'd landed in Tim and Maddie's flat, I'd realized there was one other person I could turn to for help. It was risky because she didn't officially know about my time traveling. But she'd helped me once before.

After looking her up on the internet, I'd located all of her current information. That's when I decided. If I ever needed help, I would find my friend, Natalie Bishop, whether she liked it or not.

Seeing a self-service post office kiosk on one street corner, I stopped. I knew there were very likely security cameras around, so I kept my face down and averted as I inspected my options. Thankfully, it accepted cash.

I fed the money into the machine, and it spit out some stamps. Snatching them up, I quickly walked away. A few blocks later, I took out the original letter I had written in the alley asking for Tim and Maddie's help. Without pausing to think about it or debate on whether or not this was the right time to do it, I stuck a stamp on the envelope and dropped it into a mailbox.

I didn't know for sure if I would ever travel back in time further than I was now. The important thing was, I was currently in a time before I would need to be rescued in an alley. Hopefully six months would give Tim and Maddie enough time to make their preparations. I couldn't risk waiting for a better option.

It took me a long time to walk across the city to Natalie's townhouse. I had plenty of time to think about exactly how to approach her. By the time the building was in front of me, my leg muscles were aching, my back was hurting every time I breathed, and I still didn't know exactly how to get my friend to help me.

Natalie wasn't exactly an easy target. For a long time, she had known there was something mysterious about me, but she had never asked questions and never permitted me to tell her about my time travel. She hadn't wanted to know.

Natalie's father worked at a company controlled by Katherine's family. Katherine had made certain threats, making it clear that his job would be in jeopardy if Natalie didn't cooperate in certain matters. Natalie hadn't wanted to know anything about me because she didn't want to be made to tell those secrets.

I could only hope that ten years had made a difference, in a good way. Hopefully these years had been kinder to Natalie than they had been to Wayne. From my research, I knew that Natalie wasn't married, but it looked as if she had bought the townhouse she and I had shared before I had married Seth. She still worked in the hospital, though she was now one of the most prominent OB/GYN doctors in the state.

But those were just the facts, and there was so much I still didn't know. If Natalie's father was no longer in danger, if Natalie didn't believe all of the bad things said about me, if she hadn't suffered any ill-effects from our friendship ten years ago, if she was willing to listen… then I may be able to convince her to help hide me.

Glancing around to make sure no one was watching, I ducked around the side of the stone steps to the house. I wiggled free the loose stone. Pulling the stone free, a worn key tumbled to the ground.

I smiled in weak relief. Thankfully, Natalie was a creature of habit in some respects. It had been ten years, and yet the spare house key was in the exact same hiding spot.

The key turned easily in the lock, and I cautiously entered the darkened house. I didn't expect Natalie to be home this time of day. From looking through her Facebook page, it didn't seem like she had a roommate, but I began a thorough, tiptoed inspection of the house.

I walked through the bottom floor, including the kitchen and living room, noting that Natalie had done a great job of redecorating. All of the blinds were drawn, which seemed to confirm that the house was empty for the moment.

I climbed the stairs and toured the office and the guest bedroom, which had previously been mine.

The door to Natalie's room was shut. I carefully twisted the knob and pushed, opening the door soundlessly. The room was dark with blackout curtains pulled at the window. I waited for my eyes to adjust to the dim light filtering through the open door.

Startled, I saw the bed was not empty.

Natalie lay on a mound of pillows, sound asleep.

I crept forward, peering at the dark hair cascading over my friend's face. It was somewhat a relief to find her home. Now I wouldn't have to wait. There was a chance that I had been recognized by one of the bystanders at the bakery. I needed to get Natalie on my side, and we needed a plan.

The only explanation for her being asleep at this time of day was that she had worked the night shift. I hated to wake her, but I knew I must.

"Natalie," I said, reaching out and gently shaking her shoulder. "Natalie, wake up. It's me, Hannah."

Natalie yelped and bolted upright. Screeching, she pelted me with pillows and whatever else she could find.

I put my hands in front of my face to ward off her attack, trying to make my voice penetrate her squawking panic.

She jumped out on the other side, now lobbing books at me. When an old—fashioned alarm clock hit me in the forehead, I flopped on the bed and ducked my head in the fetal position. At that point, playing dead seemed a reasonable approach .

The onslaught stopped, and Natalie's screeching reduced to whimpers.

I peeked out.

Natalie stood in her purple nightgown with mussed hair, wild eyes, and a can of pepper spray aimed my direction.

I slowly sat up with hands outstretched in surrender. "Natalie, please! It's me, Hannah!"

"What are you doing here, Hannah?" she whispered, her shaking hands still holding the pepper spray.

"I need your help. Please. I have no one else."

Natalie continued to stand, staring at me with weapon raised.

"Natalie, all the things they've said about me are lies. You know me. I would never kill Seth. I was never involved in the making of any medication for a pharmaceutical company."

Natalie swallowed and whispered. "You don't have to convince me. I never believed a word of what was said, mostly because Katherine Colson was the one saying it."

"So can you put down the pepper spray?" I asked gently.

She slowly, hesitantly lowered it to her side.

"Did your dad retire?" I asked carefully.

Her eyes lit with understanding. She knew I was really asking if I was free to confide in or if her loyalties were still divided.

"He died five years ago," she answered.

"I'm sorry, Natalie," I said, even knowing that this would mean she was free to hear my story. "I need to explain—"

"Not now, Hannah," Natalie said, holding up her hand to stop me. Looking as if she'd just come out of a trance, she threw down the pepper spray and began hurriedly rummaging through clothes.

"We can't talk now," she continued, selecting a sweater and a pair of jeans. "You aren't safe. I don't know how long you've been in the city, but someone may have recognized you. As soon as Katherine and her cronies know you're back, then they'll pay me a visit again."

"They came after you?" I asked in dread.

Natalie went into the bathroom adjoined to her bedroom and changed her clothes.

"Of course, they did," she explained, her voice drifting from the bathroom. "I was your friend. They investigated anyone who had any connection to you. But they didn't do to me what they did to Wayne. I didn't know anything, and I think that was obvious. Katherine knew she had me by threatening my dad. She knew I would have told her if I had known anything about you. So I got off easily. I wasn't made redundant like Wayne."

At my confused look, Natalie waved her hand and explained. "Made redundant—fired from your job. Seriously, Hannah, do you remember nothing I taught you?"

I covered a smile. Natalie's British accent and manner of speaking was such entertainment for me, even in the worst of situations. She had tried to teach me some of the common British slang phrases, and we'd had many hilarious conversations. But Natalie seemed to have an endless supply of British colloquialisms, and they tended to pop out more frequently when she was stressed.

"So what are we going to do?" I asked, watching Natalie as she finished stuffing clothes and toiletries in a bag.

Natalie turned off the bathroom light and walked to the door of the bedroom. She turned and looked at me. "We're going to go see a man about a dog."

CHAPTER SIXTEEN

"SO how are we going to see a man about a dog?" I asked from the passenger seat of Natalie's Volkswagen Bug. Thankfully, I had remembered that this particular British phrase could be used as an excuse when you were leaving but trying to hide your destination.

We had been driving for a while now and had just successfully crossed the Bay Bridge. Natalie already had a fast track pass, and we had thankfully not had to stop to pay a fare.

I hadn't braved a question up to this point, knowing Natalie was stressed and focused on getting out of the city. But as we traveled through the freeways of Oakland, I ventured the question.

Natalie answered, though her eyes never left the road. "There is a cabin in the mountains I get to use sometimes. It is owned by the same family friends who were my sponsors and who sold me the townhouse. But there is nothing to connect the cabin to me, or more importantly, to you. I will take you there and then come back to avoid suspicion. It's not a permanent solution, but you can stay there until you figure out how to get out of the country or how to disappear for another ten years."

"Natalie, I need to tell you what's going on." I said firmly.

"No you don't," she said quickly. "Like I told you years ago, I don't want to know anything."

"But with your dad gone…"

"But Katherine isn't gone. Like I said, as soon as they know you're back in the area, they will come to me. The less I know about you, the better. Look what they did to Wayne and to your family. They can't make me tell what I don't know."

I couldn't hide the crestfallen look from my face. I still couldn't confide in Natalie, which meant she wouldn't help me more than by taking me to the cabin. She didn't want to be involved, and I couldn't blame her. The risk to her own life was too great.

Even now, the thought of what would happen to Timmy and Maddie if I didn't change the future sent shivers down my spine. Six months from now, I would jump out the window and disappear. They would be apprehended and interrogated. Or worse.

So much depended on me changing the future, but once Natalie left me at that cabin, I would once again be completely alone. I had been abandoned by everyone. Even God seemed to be turning a blind eye to me, not that I had asked for anything different. Yet for the briefest of seconds, I longed to be able to call out to Him.

But I had shut that door, and instead of standing at the door knocking, I had the awful feeling that He had left me too.

I spoke quietly, to no one in particular. "So I guess that's it. And Bob's your uncle." One of Natalie's favorite sayings just slipped off my tongue. A phrase simply meaning, 'and that's that,' seemed the best way to express the finality of the situation

Natalie sighed. "Hannah, don't be upset. I'm not a daft cow. I haven't seen you in donkey's years and yet you look exactly the same as the last time I saw you. Remember, we had lunch together a few days before Seth died and you disappeared. I think you even have that same bruise on your upper arm. Didn't you say you hit it on a file cabinet that Seth left open at work? I'm not an idiot. But if you tell me, then everything will be real. It could throw a spanner in the works that would make my life look like Wayne's."

I felt a ridiculous giggle bubbling up at the numerous British colloquialisms Natalie had just used. A stressed Natalie could be almost unintelligible. But even that simple truth let me know that though she wouldn't help me further than the cabin, she still cared about me.

"I understand, Natalie," I said. "And please don't feel like I blame you at all. I appreciate you helping me and wouldn't want to put you in any more danger. Enough people have been hurt because of me."

"Hannah, I don't think you understand. You want to tell me so I can support you in what you're going through. But I already trust and believe you. I will help you all I can, but I don't have to know more than I already do. I know what's important. I know that you're innocent. I know that you're my friend. And I know that by helping you, I will be opposing Katherine Colson. I'm all for anything that has the potential to stop that evil woman."

Without waiting for a response, Natalie reached out and turned up the volume on the radio. She had periodically been checking the news reports about every fifteen minutes. I assumed she was listening to hear if there were any reports of me.

We listened to the innocuous report, followed by the weather. Once over, Natalie reached out and turned the volume back down.

"It looks like we might be in the clear," I said.

Natalie's eyes drifted up to the rearview mirror. "I'm less worried about the news report and more concerned about the SUV that seems to be following us."

I turned around and looked. There was a dark SUV a few car lengths back.

"What makes you think it's following us?"

"It never changes lanes," Natalie said grimly. "I've slowed down purposely, yet it stays the same distance behind us, even while every other car on the road whips past."

"But if they knew I was here, wouldn't it be on the news?" I asked, trying not to panic.

"No," Natalie said flatly. "We're talking about Katherine. If she knew you were here, she would keep it as quiet as possible as long as possible. She wouldn't want to publicly bring you in, she wants to do it quietly. She doesn't want a media storm. She wants to be able to do with you as she wishes."

Dread settled in the pit of my stomach. "I had a rather unfortunate arrival at a bakery before I went to your house," I admitted. "I didn't have my hat and sunglasses on. They probably had a security camera."

Natalie's voice continued calmly, but she had a death-grip on the steering wheel. "If they spotted you, then they would have checked with Wayne and me immediately. We are your closest associates that are still alive. They keep close tabs on us. Every once in a while, I notice someone watching me. When I wasn't at my house this afternoon, they would have tracked down my car."

"So what are we going to do?" I asked, my mind running through possible scenarios. "If those are really Katherine's goons behind us, then why aren't they trying to force us off the road and apprehend me?"

"They probably don't know for sure it's you, and they don't want to cause a scene if they don't have to. They're waiting for an opportunity. My guess is that they will use the tunnel up ahead. They'll close the road behind us. Another car will block the exit. We'll never make it out."

"Then what are we going to do?" I asked, alarm threading my voice as I strained forward to see the road ahead.

The tunnel was less than a mile away!

"We don't go in the tunnel," Natalie said

matter-of-factly.

Natalie took the next exit off the freeway.

"Hold on, Hannah," she gritted out as she made a quick turn at the end of the off-ramp. "I've got to try to give us some distance through several lights. Then we'll have to park the car and run. We'll have to get some other means of transportation."

"You might want to close your eyes!" Natalie added as she accelerated through the first red light.

My friend knew my fear of driving in a car, but I knew I couldn't be reduced to a spineless blob. I needed to help her.

I turned around and watched the SUV swerve through several cars that had entered the intersection after we had crossed it. There was no question. They were definitely following us, and now they realized we were onto them.

As Natalie swerved around corners and through lights and stop signs, I managed to give her progress reports. When the SUV had disappeared from view for about a minute, Natalie pulled the Bug into a strip mall and hopped out.

"We have to find a bus or other vehicle," Natalie said.

But before we'd gotten ten steps from the car, we saw a different SUV whiz around the corner from the opposite direction.

"Run!" Natalie shouted.

We ran to a storefront and pulled the door open. It was an import store, filled to the brim with imported decorations, furniture, and knickknacks from around the world.

"There has to be a back exit," I said, as Natalie and I filtered through the menagerie to the back of the store.

The proprietor was a Chinese woman who smiled and nodded happily to us as we passed.

There was indeed a door at the back with an old exit sign over it.

"There is no doorknob," Natalie hissed incredulously, trying instead to push at the door with her weight.

But it had been boarded up in what had to be a clear building code violation.

"We can't get out!" I said, pulling Natalie back as she moved to kick at the unyielding wood planks.

I pulled her back toward the front door. Maybe those in the SUV hadn't seen which store we entered. Maybe we could escape out the front.

Before we'd gotten halfway back through the store, the front door opened and two men in suits entered.

"Quick, hide!" I whispered.

Natalie crawled under a highly-polished coffee table. I hunched back against the wall concealing myself behind a coat rack full of elaborate fans and fancy hats from around the world.

I held my breath, not daring to breathe as the two men strolled leisurely through the store. They spoke a friendly greeting to the proprietor and made a thorough examination of all the shop had to offer.

I watched around the edge of a fan as they came closer. My heart thudded painfully, and I was suddenly very light-headed. They were going to find us! With as thorough as they were being, there was no way they wouldn't locate our hiding places. They knew we were in the store and were simply taking their time to find us.

I shrank as far back as I could. One of the men headed in the direction of Natalie's table while the other one made his way toward me. Closer and closer he came. He picked up a Russian nesting doll, examined it, and put it back.

He was five feet away. Four feet.

Movement caught my eye. Natalie stuck her foot out and tripped the guy near her. As he hit the floor, taking out a display of international soaps, she rolled out from under the table, sprang to her feet, and sprinted for the door, screaming at the top of her lungs. The man who was near me took off after her.

But instead of running as fast as she could, I saw Natalie glance behind her shoulder, checking to see that the man was following her. She flung the door open and raced out into the afternoon, taking off in a direction away from the front door.

I suddenly realized what she was doing. She had sacrificed herself for me. She was trying to provide a distraction so that I could escape. As the man chased her out of the store, I peeked around the fan, trying to find the man Natalie had tripped. The proprietor stood at the front door, leaning out to watch the chase. I inched forward, scanning the entire area from the front door to the coffee table.

He was nowhere in sight.

I stepped back and swiveled to scan the other end of the shop.

But instead, I came face to face with a man in a suit.

I startled and backed up, knocking over the coat rack in my haste.

The man grabbed both of my hands in a vice-like grip. The corner of his mouth cocked in a satisfied grin. He reached out and pulled off my stocking cap, releasing my red hair to tumble around me.

His foul breath washed over me with one word.

"Boo."

CHAPTER SEVENTEEN

NATALIE and I huddled together in the back of the SUV, trying to ignore two guns pointed directly at us.

"Nice and easy, girls," The suit sitting in the backseat with us said as the vehicle started. He looked at me, a light of triumph in his eyes. "We have someone important who has been looking for you a long time."

Natalie and I remained quiet. I felt her tension. It was one thing that I had been apprehended, but I couldn't stand that Natalie had been caught as well and would now face consequences for her association with me.

After the man had grabbed me in the shop, I had fought. Maddie would have been proud. I would have gotten away if a reinforcement of suits hadn't arrived. Three men had carried me to an SUV. My only consolation was that all of them would likely scar from the bites and scratches I'd managed to inflict. The guy from the shop had gotten the worst. He'd probably needed a hospital visit for a concussion after I had landed a kick to his gut that had sent him sailing into a golden Buddha statue.

When they shoved me in, all the fight drained out of me the instant I saw Natalie hunched in the corner of the leather-seated SUV. Three of the suits rode in the vehicle with us, while the others piled into their own vehicle. One suit rode in the front passenger side, but he was turned around to the back, keeping his eyes and his gun trained on Natalie and me.

The other suit sat in the back with us, keeping his gun aimed at us as well, but what was almost more concerning to me was the fact that he had my backpack in his lap. After getting in the vehicle, he had gone through it, probably checking for weapons. Thankfully, I had made some upgrades to the backpack in the past month. Maddie had helped me create hidden pockets to store my cash and the medications. That way, if the bag ever got searched, as it was now, then the important items wouldn't be discovered.

The suit unloaded everything in the main compartment of the backpack, but of course, he didn't find anything particularly interesting.

"Make sure you put all of that junk back in her bag," the driver ordered. "You know who will want to see it."

The SUV got back on the freeway, headed back toward San Francisco.

"I think we're snookered, Hannah," Natalie whispered. "We need to figure out how to throw a spanner in the works."

My terrified mind tried to translate what Natalie was

saying. I knew she was purposely speaking British-ese, hoping that I would be the only one to understand. If my British slang knowledge was correct, then she was saying that we were in a bad situation and needed to figure out how to mess up the plan.

Before I could nod my understanding, the suit in the front seat waved his gun and barked, "Stop whispering. Remember, I have a gun. We've been warned about you. If you try anything, I'm not afraid to shoot."

My throat constricted in fear, but Natalie's whisper was at my ear once again. "Don't listen to him, Hannah. You're dead now, or you're dead when Katherine gets a hold of you. Which would be worse?"

My eyes shot to hers and the memories of countless nightmares filled my mind. I'd had vivid nightmares almost every night for the past month. Awful images were seared in my mind of seeing my parents and Abby tortured while I watched, helpless to save them. It didn't matter that I had never actually experienced the memories; they were real in every other possible way. They were really enough to wake myself screaming, and they were powerful enough to cause my body to tremble and my breath to grow short, even now.

I'd never been brave. Natalie on the other hand, was brave enough to be reckless, but she was smart enough to not take a stupid risk.

I nodded. "What do we do?"

"Stop talking!" the suit whispered again. His eyes shot back and forth wildly between the two of us. He wouldn't be as scary if his gun arm didn't have a long, elaborate tattoo of skulls running the length of it.

"Please," Natalie said in her most vulnerable voice. "Don't hurt us. I was only telling her that I really needed to use the loo. I'm not sure I can hold it."

"The loo?" The other suit beside us grunted.

"The bathroom," I clarified. "She needs to use the bathroom.

"There is no way I'm stopping," the suit driving the car said. "That's the oldest trick in the book."

"Natalie," I said, keeping my voice soft, but loud enough to be heard by everyone in the car. "Did you forget to wear your Depends?"

Natalie looked at me in misery—an Oscar worthy performance. "I don't usually wear them on days I don't work!"

"She has a medical condition," I said, turning to the suits. "When she says she has to go, she really does. She's had some unfortunate accidents."

Natalie groaned, "I really have to go!"

"That one in the movie theater was so embarrassing," I said, looking at my friend worriedly. I didn't know where I was coming up with this stuff, or even if the ruse would work, but the suits were definitely looking uncomfortable.

"I have to go NOW!" Natalie wailed.

"Pull over!" the suit beside us ordered. "There's a gas station right off the next exit.

"I am not going to pull over!" the driver yelled. "Let her pee all over!"

"This isn't your car, Driscoll," The suit yelled back. "And you aren't the one who will have to sit back here with pee over everything."

Natalie continued wailing while the men argued.

"Enough!" the tattooed suit boomed above the noise. "I'll just shoot her now. Then she won't pee all over, and we'll be done with her! She's not the important one anyway."

He cocked his gun, aiming it at Natalie's chest!

"No!" I panicked, trying to push Natalie out of the way and shielding her with my own body.

The next few seconds were chaos.

The tires screeched. The car swerved.

The tattooed suit turned back around to the front. "Watch out!" he bellowed.

The car swerved again and again. There was screaming and then the jolt of impact. My ears were filled with the sounds of cracking glass and the crunch of metal. I was thrust forward, but the seatbelt caught me.

In the sudden silence, I heard moaning from the front seat. Like me, Natalie was unharmed and quickly removed her seat belt. Reaching up to the seat in front of us, she carefully hit the unlock button for the doors.

"What just happened?" The suit in the back seat groaned.

"So many cars," we heard the driver mumble. "Where did they come from?"

"Idiot!" The tattooed suit growled from the front seat. "You headed down the wrong way on the freeway."

"I did not!" the driver shot back. "One minute ago, everyone was headed the other direction. Then cars just suddenly appeared, headed straight at us!"

I felt Natalie reach around me and grab something off the floor. She nodded at me, her hand on the door handle. It was now or never. The suits were growing more coherent and emergency vehicles would be here within minutes. The SUV had been hit on the front driver's side. Thankfully, it had been more sideswipe than head-on. Even now, people were starting to walk up to the vehicle and peer inside, checking to see the status of the passengers.

Natalie opened the door and flung herself out. I turned, grabbed my backpack from where it had fallen against the seat, and launched myself after her.

As soon as our feet hit the pavement, I heard shouts and the click of car doors opening behind us. After only about twenty paces away from the SUV, I knew we weren't going to make it. Traffic was stopped behind us with only one lane still going through. We were running forward along the freeway, but there was no place to hide. The suits would catch us or we would be hit by one of the cars still filtering through the accident.

I turned around and looked over my shoulder as I ran. Two of the suits were out of the SUV and running after us while the driver looked to be trying to restart the damaged vehicle. From my brief glance, I saw that the two men on foot were limping and struggling in pursuit. I was more worried about the SUV. The front on the driver's side had crashed into the barrier, probably when our driver had swerved to avoid hitting an oncoming vehicle. But it didn't look severely damaged. We could outrun the suits on foot, but not the one in the car.

We needed a way to get off the freeway fast.

"Natalie," I choked out, motioning her to follow me.

I ran to the one lane still allowing traffic. In the distance, I heard the sirens of emergency vehicles.

The lane was moving slowly. Without hesitation, I stepped in front of the next oncoming vehicle. The silver sports car stopped, and the driver rolled down the window.

"Please," I said desperately. "We need your help. We're being chased."

The middle-aged man startled and began rolling up his window.

"Get out of the car," Natalie said firmly, and her words were punctuated by a strange click.

I turned to see a gun in Natalie's hand, and it was pointed confidently at the driver.

The man's eyes flew wide, and he hurried to open the door.

"Natalie, what are you doing?" I squeaked.

"Getting us out of here. Get in!" she ordered as the

man moved out of the way.

Seeing that the suits were rapidly closing the gap, I obediently ran around and jumped into the passenger side.

Natalie pressed the accelerator right as the tattooed suit pounded on the window. His fist fell away harmlessly as the sports car's tires squealed in sudden acceleration.

"Natalie, I can't believe you just stole a car!" I was practically hyperventilating. In all of my time traveling, I had managed to never commit a crime... until now. "Where did you get that gun?"

"That guy in the back with us wasn't using it," Natalie said with a nonchalant shrug. "It fell down when we hit the barrier, so I swiped it up before we jumped out."

Natalie took the next freeway exit and turned so she could swing around and go the opposite direction, toward San Francisco.

"Where are we going?" I asked nervously.

"I have no idea." Natalie replied. "I just thought we'd head west since the bad guys would probably guess us to try to head the other way, like we did before. I was hoping you might be able to give us a destination. I think it's pretty obvious that we aren't in Kansas anymore."

Despite the chaotic confusion of the last few minutes, deep down I already knew what had happened. The time had finally come when the truth was unavoidable for Natalie and me. I had to tell her everything, yet suddenly

I couldn't find the words.

"Let me tell you what I know," Natalie said, filling in my silence. "A few years ago, they completely reconstructed this section of freeway. They built a new westbound section which replaced the old, deteriorated one. Then they rerouted the traffic and made the old westbound lanes eastbound."

"So traffic went the opposite direction of what it had previously."

"Yes," Natalie confirmed. "So tell me how that is possible," she prodded.

I sighed wearily. "In the next few years I guess they'll reconstruct this freeway, and it'll be exactly as it was ten minutes ago. I can't tell you how it is possible because it is actually very impossible."

After getting on the freeway, Natalie had slowed way down. With the immediate danger past, the sense of urgency wasn't as great. Instead, she drove only slightly faster than the rest of the traffic. After all, we were in a stolen car. It was probably best to get wherever we were going as quickly as we could without attracting any undue attention.

"Time travel?" Natalie asked. Her tone was hushed but not in the least bit shocked. "I can't say that the wild thought hadn't crossed my mind over the years, but I don't think I would have ever believed it if there hadn't suddenly been cars headed straight toward us, the opposite of what they had been seconds before. But, how?"

"I time travel when my emotions get extreme," I

explained. "If I am touching someone or something else, then that person or thing comes with me. Since I was in the SUV, it and all of its passengers travelled through time with me."

"Hannah, this is mad!"

"I know," I said. "My time traveling is caused—"

Natalie held up a hand to stop my words. "I don't need to know the scientific details, I just need to know how we get back. We don't have time. If we're really in the past, we can't stay here."

Dread suddenly filled Natalie's face. "Oh no! What are we going to do about Katherine's goons? They came back with us. We can't exactly leave them here in the past, and I'm not excited about the idea of finding them so you can touch them back to the future."

"It doesn't work that way," I said, a tiny laugh bubbling up at her word choice. "Everything that traveled with me should go back to its original time when I travel again. At least that's what has happened before. I shouldn't need to be touching any of the other travelers for the return trip. It's like everything returns to its original time stamp.

"Okay, so take us back," Natalie said. "We got away from the bad guys. Take us back to the right time."

"I can't," I said miserably. "I can't control it. I never know what will cause me to time travel. I can get really upset and not travel, or I can just feel really happy and leap back in time. I can't do it when I want to, no matter how much I try."

"Hannah, you have to," Natalie said urgently. "Katherine's goons will go to her and the authorities. They'll figure out they're in the wrong time! I can't imagine the consequences for everyone, especially you. We don't even know when we are. What if one of those guys really screws up history?"

"I know, Natalie! But there isn't anything I can do. I didn't plan on time traveling. Everything just happened, and then we were going down the wrong way on a five lane freeway!"

"Well, you don't have a choice. We have nowhere to—"

Natalie let out a strangled scream and swerved to the right.

I looked out her side window and saw a muddy, green Ford truck.

"He tried to hit us!" Natalie sputtered.

I watched as the truck drove parallel to us. Craning my neck, I looked through its window and saw a familiar face.

"Natalie, it's the guy with the tattoo!

Natalie looked up to her rearview mirror. "It's worse than that. He isn't our only company."

I turned around and saw an SUV with a smashed front driver's side coming up behind us.

Natalie and I had been so focused talking that we hadn't paid attention to the possibility of being followed. We thought we had escaped. It didn't occur to me that the suits might have been able to launch a chase.

And now it was too late.

The truck swerved toward us again, Natalie accelerated. Though the corvette we were in would easily outdistance the other two cars, we were too late. We were boxed in with the green truck on our left, The SUV behind, and traffic in front.

Seeing an opening, Natalie accelerated, narrowly managing to swerve past a minivan and in front of the truck. Now a mini Cooper was in front of us, and the truck and SUV resumed their positions boxing us in.

"We're not going to make it!" Natalie gritted out. "I'm going to change lanes and hit the brakes hard. We'll probably be hit. When we stop, you jump out and run."

"I can't leave you, Natalie!" I refused adamantly.

"You have to! You're the only one who can get me out of this mess, and I don't know that you can do that if you're caught."

I knew what she was referring to. "I don't know that I can time travel, Natalie," I whispered. "What if I can't? I can't leave you. What will happen to you?"

"You have to leave me, and you have to time travel. Please, Hannah. I can buy you some time, but you're the one who has to do the rescuing."

My heart felt like it was twisting inside my chest, but I knew she was right. "Okay," I consented softly.

"Get ready."

"Wait! Not yet!" I hurriedly opened my backpack and

rummaged around for one of the hidden pockets. Finding it, I pulled out some of the medication that had been labeled with Seth's name. It was complete with instructions, which Seth had presumably prepared in case he'd been unable to administer the medication himself.

I handed some of the medication to Natalie along with the instructions. "When you get back to your own time, you have to follow these instructions and give yourself this medication. The injection comes immediately and then the pills."

"Okay, okay," Natalie said impatiently. "They're going to try to ram us again. I have to try this now!"

"Natalie, this is important. You have to take this medication or you will die!"

Natalie jerked the wheel to the right and slammed on her brakes. The SUV hit us from behind, catching the left corner in a sickening crunch of metal. The corvette fishtailed in a full, dizzying circle, stopping only when the driver's side swiped past the concrete barrier then hit the green truck.

"Go, Hannah! Go!" Natalie yelled as soon as motion stopped.

I had no time to feel, react, or even check myself for injuries. I looked at Natalie, hoping she could make a run for it with me, but the truck was blocking her door. With one last tortured glance at my friend, I threw open the door and ran.

I ran across traffic, starting and stopping to the music of vehicles' squealing brakes. The accident was already mostly on the shoulder, so three of the lanes were still moving, but with rubberneckers who were more interested in the accident than in paying attention to where they themselves were going.

I climbed over a cement barrier that was about waist-high and ran up a green hill on the other side. I was out of breath from both exertion and anxiety when I reached the top. A shopping center lay before me at the bottom of the hill.

I turned back around, checking my pursuers. There was only one suit trying to cross the lanes of traffic without much success. While I watched, two different cars almost hit him.

Natalie was nowhere in sight, but since the two other suits were gathered around the corvette, I assumed she was still inside, biding her time.

A sob escaped my throat. I felt ill. Nausea came in waves, and it felt as if a knife was twisting into my chest.

Earlier I had left Maddie and Timmy. I had abandoned them. Because of their involvement with me, they would face an unknown fate, and the blame would belong to me. Now I had abandoned Natalie as well. They would all possibly face torture and death because of me.

I looked down at the scene with a sense of complete guilt and hopelessness. The dark SUV was behind the silver corvette. The green truck, with its thick layer of dirt still intact was at a slight angle away from the sports car.

I caught my breath. An eerie sense of déjà vu trickled down my spine. There was something very familiar about this scene. I had seen that same Corvette and that same mud-encrusted Ford truck before.

I drew the memory out like a long string. Same vehicle damage. Slightly different positions. When I had seen the accident, both vehicles had been pushed to the side. The SUV hadn't been there. It was just the truck and the car.

Suddenly startled, I brought my hand to my mouth.

I remembered *when*.

Five years after I had saved the Lawson family, Seth and I had re-met, and he had taken me to visit the family I had rescued. On the way back from their house, we had gotten delayed due to the traffic from an accident. As we had passed the cause of the traffic jam, I joined other rubberneckers in gawking at the scene.

It was *this* scene.

The instant full recognition dawned with a startling jolt, I saw it all disappear in a shimmer.

CHAPTER EIGHTEEN

I stood in the shadow of the bakery and looked up. My stomach twisted. I shouldn't be here. But I had nowhere else to go.

When the car accident scene in front of me had disappeared, I knew I had time traveled. But I was alone. I could only hope that Natalie and the suits had made it back to their own time, while I had apparently landed sometime else.

I didn't know where to go. I had no one left to help me. It didn't matter when I was; I had burned through what friends I had left and was now utterly alone.

As if on autopilot, I took my stocking cap and sunglasses out of where the suit had stuck them in the backpack. I mechanically made my way through the shopping center parking lot and to the BART station beyond.

I paid the fare to get to San Francisco and boarded the

transit train. Thankfully, BART passengers tended to keep to themselves. At least I hoped that was the case. I found a corner in the back and hunched down, hoping I appeared standoffish enough to ward off any friendlies.

I glanced down at the date on my ticket stub. Somehow I was not surprised to see I was back to the same date I had started the morning at.

The trip into the city was blessedly uneventful. After arriving in San Francisco, I had spent several hours hunched in an alley waiting for dark. Though I had a lot of time to think, I still had no plan even after the sun had long set. I had eventually started wandering and ended up here, back where I had started the day—at Tim and Maddie's flat.

I stared up at the darkened windows of the flat that had been home for the last month. I had to know if Maddie and Tim were okay. I had watched the news on a TV while riding BART, expecting to see some major coverage of what had happened at the flat earlier. But nothing was mentioned.

Maybe Tim and Maddie had been interrogated and released. Maybe they were safe, asleep in their beds. There was no one loitering around the outside of the building and no vehicles parked in the vicinity. Katherine's men had likely cleared out hours ago. Even if Tim and Maddie were gone, the flat might be the safest place for me. After all, no one would expect me to return to the place I'd barely escaped from earlier.

With all that considered, I couldn't walk away, not without knowing for sure about Tim and Maddie.

I pulled myself up on the fire escape and quickly climbed to the top, trying to keep my footfalls as softly as possible on the metal steps. Reaching the door, I slid the key in that I'd been clutching in my hand for the past few minutes. Though I hadn't understood at the time, I was glad that Tim had insisted I put a spare key to the flat in my backpack.

I opened the door with the softest of creaks and tiptoed in. I walked through the dark hallway and saw a soft glow coming from the living room.

Timmy?

My heart quickened. Was he really here and working late at night, just like usual?

My pace quickened. I stepped into the large room with anxious eyes zeroing immediately in on the light.

I froze. My heart stopped along with my breath, and I wasn't sure either one would ever start again.

The lone light illuminated a woman sitting relaxed in my favorite leather chair.

Katherine.

Her eyes brightened in surprise and a slow, satisfied smile lifted her lips.

"Well, this is unexpected," she said, her voice husky and almost lazy. "But I can't say that I'm not absolutely thrilled to see you, Hannah. It's been a long time… at least for me. Maybe not for you."

I let my glare give my reply for me.

An instinctive part of me urged me to turn around and

run. But I was tired of running. In some respects, I had been searching for Katherine as she had been searching for me. She was the only one who knew the truth. She was the one who had created this mess of a future. If I intended to fix things, I was going to have to deal with her at some point.

"Come on in, Hannah. Sit down so we can talk a bit."

"No thank you," I gritted out, folding my arms across myself. "I'd rather stand."

"Suit yourself," Katherine said easily, standing herself and extending her body in a delicate little stretch. "I can honestly say I wasn't expecting company this evening. I couldn't come earlier, of course. The governor of California can't be seen around such an incident, especially since we're rather reluctant to include the media. I just wanted to see where you had been living, Hannah, to get a feel for you and maybe a few clues as to where you would go next. Then, lo and behold, the woman comes in the flesh!"

Her sweet tone and conciliatory manner were sickening and about more than I could take. This wasn't a social call. I wanted answers.

"Where are Tim and Maddie?" I demanded.

Katherine just smiled, as if perfectly content to keep her secrets and stay in control.

"You put on quite a performance six months ago," she said instead. "A couple of my men still haven't fully recovered. Fortunately, we were able to save their lives, but only because Wayne was persuaded to help."

Amanda Tru

"Natalie?" I asked, almost involuntarily. If Katherine's men had made it back in time six months ago, then Natalie should have as well. But that also meant she would have had the same deadly effects from time traveling. I had given her the medication, but that was no guarantee she had taken it and lived.

Katherine's eyes lit with interest. "Natalie Bishop disappeared around that same time. We weren't sure if she made a reappearance at the same time as my men, but if she did, then she was no longer available for contact. There was some speculation that she had gone to Mexico. You obviously expected her to be here and seem almost afraid that she shared the same fate as the others. That's rather interesting. Maybe we need to be a bit more thorough in our investigation."

I masked a sigh of relief. The mention of Mexico gave me hope that Natalie was alive and Wayne had helped her flee the country. But Katherine had also said that Wayne had helped save the men who had time traveled with me. She had used the word 'persuaded.'

With a sharp intake of breath, I realized that something could have happened to Wayne. If I had altered the last six months, then Wayne may not have been there to help me at the dealership and the ferry.

My brow furrowed in concentration, and I searched my memories, looking for anything new that hadn't been there earlier in the day.

Wayne would have never told me about Natalie or anything else that may have happened six months ago. From his initial questions, he would have known that none of that would have happened yet for me, and he would have stayed quiet. Thankfully, even with the mess that had happened, it didn't seem to change any of my experience with Wayne on the ferry. Everything, down to that awful kiss, had been the same, at least according to my recollection. None of the memories varied from the originals.

I looked up to find a fascinated and yet amused expression on Katherine's face as she studied me.

"It must be a bit confusing to try to keep everything straight after a while," she said, as if she had been able to read the direction of my thoughts.

"There are some things that are constant," I replied easily. "For instance, you are always evil."

Katherine laughed, the tinkling sound bubbling across the room. "Ouch! That's pretty harsh, especially when you're talking about someone who has always strived for the greater good. Sometimes that requires a little individual inconvenience."

"It's your definition of 'individual inconvenience' that I find unacceptable and downright evil," I shot back.

There would be no reasoning with her. To me, she seemed a deluded psychopath, and there was no arguing with such a person. It was obvious that Katherine wasn't going to provide any information about Natalie, and if she also wasn't willing to answer about Maddie and Tim, then maybe I should just leave.

I wasn't going to beat her today; any of my battles would have to be won in the past.

Of course she would try to stop me from leaving, but

there was a reason Maddie taught me self-defense. And I had to admit, the thought of getting to use some moves on Katherine gave me a bit of a thrill. Unfortunately, I realized that besting her now would in no way change history or my current desperate situation.

Then it hit me. This might be the chance I was looking for. If I could get information out of Katherine now, it might give me the edge I needed to beat her in the past and change things. With sudden certainty, I knew this was the turning point. It almost felt like we were two opposing forces meeting for the last time. One of us would come out the victor.

"I'll make you a deal, Katherine," I said confidently. "How about you answer two questions for me, and then I will answer whatever two questions you want to ask me."

Katherine looked at me like I was an amusing child. "If that's the game you want to play, then let's do it," she said, sitting back down on the chair. Her ankles crossed delicately. Her blond hair shone softly in the lamplight. Even at this late hour, her makeup was in perfect condition, and she was dressed in a designer, gray business suit.

It was rather disappointing to see that the stress of her political ambitions and success hadn't aged her.

She looked at me expectantly, as if entertained by the thought of humoring the child.

"Where are Tim and Maddie?" I asked again.

"They are safe, for now. We have them in custody, though so far they are being quite unhelpful where you're concerned." She flashed me a smile. "Next."

I swallowed. Her answer hadn't really helped me except to know that Tim and Maddie were alive but hadn't escaped today's attack.

My mind whirled with possibilities for my next question. This was the last one, so there was a lot of pressure. This was the question that could determine whether I changed history and saved Seth, my family, Wayne, and everyone else.

"How did you know?" I asked quietly. "Seth was shot on December 20. The next year, you were there waiting for us. You took Wayne into custody and probably Abby and my parents as well. How did you know we would show up then?"

Katherine gave a soft, amused, little laugh. "Out of all the questions you could ask, that's what you want to know? I'm surprised, Hannah! I think I've given you more credit than you deserve in the area of intelligence. That one was relatively easy."

I worked hard to remain calm. I didn't want to give Katherine the satisfaction of a reaction. My fingers flexed with tension, but I tried to focus, waiting for her answer.

Sighing dramatically, she began her story in a weary, almost singsong voice. "Earlier that same day—December 19th—the men working for me and Jones-Stanton tracked you to an Orchard Supply Hardware store in Sonora. They found your SUV there, but not you. Of course, they took the liberty of searching your vehicle, but they didn't really need to. The registration sticker on your license plate read December of the following year. Oddly, your SUV seemed to disappear right about the time I saw you and Seth vanish from the pier. But that didn't matter. After what I'd seen and heard over the years, I came up with a few conjectures. After all, you've always seemed to appear and disappear at the oddest times. I knew you and Seth would very likely show up again, and since your vehicle had apparently come from a year later, I made the guess that you would return from where you came. The exact date and time were educated guesses, but exactly one year later almost seemed a bit poetic. Of course, I'd had men waiting at Fort Baker Pier every night of December, just in case, but I came along for the show on December 20th."

My heart sank. Katherine was right; that was rather obvious and thoroughly unhelpful information. And it did me absolutely no good. I couldn't go back and prevent that SUV from being found. I couldn't prevent Katherine from finding out about the registration sticker.

I was still no closer to having a plan to go back, save Seth, and fix the timeline.

"Now, if I remember correctly, you're supposed to answer two questions for me." Katherine leaned forward, her eyes shining brightly.

My throat constricted, and I couldn't swallow. Katherine would not likely waste her questions.

She paused, staring at me, obviously enjoying my discomfort. The silence lengthened to an almost palpable tension.

Katherine suddenly sat back and smiled. "Actually,

I'm going to give you a pass. You see, there is not a single question I need to ask you that I don't already have the answer to. And any other curiosities I have… well, I have ways to figure them out, with or without your consent. Of course, the 'without your consent' part is the one that's going to be fun."

Adrenaline raced from my head to my feet like fire.

I had to get out of there now!

But before I could move, I felt a prick to the back of my neck. The room instantly became fuzzy and cartoonish. I felt my knees buckle. A warmth spread through my body like a puddle. I melted to the floor.

The last thing I heard was the sound of Katherine's laughter.

CHAPTER NINETEEN

I awoke to quiet beeps and a steady dripping sound.

My nose itched. I went to reach up and scratch it. But I couldn't move. My hand felt pinned down. I tried my other hand. It couldn't move either.

My eyes flew open wide. I tried to sit up and couldn't. Panic raced through me. I tried to turn my head, but it was immobilized as well. I was tied down to a hard metal table and couldn't move a single part of my body.

My eyes dashed around my field of vision. I could see an IV drip and some medical instruments on my right. To my left I saw a familiar lighting fixture. I was in Tim and Maddie's flat.

Claustrophobia beckoned. I couldn't move. Why was I here? I clearly remembered my conversation with Katherine, including her ominous last words to me. Then I must have been injected with a sedative.

My breathing grew shallow. What was she going to

do to me?

"Oh, good! You're awake," a male voice said brightly.

A man with a fringe of white hair and glasses appeared above me.

"What—"

"Shhh, you don't have to say anything," he carefully laid a piece of duct tape across my mouth. "We'll find out everything we need to know. Miss Colson asked me to tell you she is sorry she couldn't stay. She had some important business at the capitol, but will come check in when she can. So let's get started! Then we'll surely have some exciting results when the governor comes back!"

My eyes were wide. I tried to catch his gaze. I wanted to beg him to not do this, even if only with a glance, but he kept his eyes to his task, humming lightly in between a casual monologue.

"This isn't the ideal laboratory, of course. We've had to make do. Miss Colson didn't want to risk any attention from moving you, so we decided to just set up camp here. A table, a few boxes of equipment, a nice investment to the baker downstairs, and we're all set!"

He began hooking me up to some equipment. Electrodes went on my head in specific spots. An automatic blood pressure cuff was placed on my arm. Other instruments were also readied to monitor my heart rate and temperature.

The man turned to a computer screen. His humming paused. "So I'm told you have a rather unique ability.

I've already done some blood and DNA analysis. I've found some very interesting data. You are a fascinating case. What I don't know is how the time travel works. I have noticed unique brain chemistry in some of your scans. You seem to have a deadly amount of tempamine, which is impossible, of course. My theory is that this has something to do with your ability. What I'm going to do is to try to artificially raise and lower the levels in the brain. Of course, we'll start small I don't want you to actually time travel. But if I can control the levels, then we can move on to the next step."

Tears welled up in my eyes and spilled down my face like the tracks of rain on a window pane. I felt violated, terrified, and so very helpless. This mad scientist had done tests on me while I'd been unconscious. Now he was going to perform experiments. He seemed to have no care of me except as a medical specimen. To him, I wasn't human.

He glanced at me and let out a giddy chuckle. "I know, now you're wondering what the next step is. Of course, after we control *when* you time travel, then we will work on controlling *where* you go. You'll also start sessions right away with Dr. Azod. He will be working on developing your wants and desires to be for the greater good. In the end, we're very hopeful that you will serve Miss Colson, your country, and the world by going back in time to specific dates where, with a few simple actions, you can prevent tragedies from ever happening."

I wanted to scream! They were going to try to brainwash me!

The mad scientist began humming again as he

refocused on his final preparations.

With the tape on my mouth, I couldn't breathe. I flexed against the restraints, hoping that one of them would be loose. But they held me tight and immobile

I had a powerful urge to reach up and touch my locket, to make sure it was still around my neck, offering hope that time would work out the way it was supposed to. But I couldn't even wiggle my hand to fight for that simple reassurance. The locket may as well have been gone, and with it, all hope was gone too.

Oh, God, no!

I couldn't remember the last time I'd said an actual, coherent prayer.

I closed my eyes, begging myself to time travel somewhere, anywhere. But I could still hear the man's humming. Nothing changed.

I heard his feet shuffle. "Almost ready," he muttered.

I began naming the elements of the periodic table. *Hydrogen, Helium, Lithium, Beryllium…*

It wasn't working! The fear and panic were still rising, strangling me in their intensity.

I could recite pi! *3.1415926535897932384626…* I stopped. What came next, was it a 4 or a 3? I normally could remember more than that! Was it a 4 or a 3?

Deep in thought, my eyes slit open and caught sight of the man holding up a large syringe for inspection.

Oh, God, please! This can't be happening!

My sobs shook the restraints.

I had no hope. Seth and my family were dead. Everyone else had been apprehended. I didn't even know what had happened to Natalie. I had lost everything.

O Lord, You have searched me and known me.

You know my sitting down and my rising up;

You understand my thoughts afar off.

I had only wanted to save my sister. I had been so desperate to save her that I hadn't cared about God's plan. I knew what had to be done.

Where can I go from Your Spirit?

Or where can I flee from Your presence?

If I ascend into heaven, You are there;

If I make my bed in hell, behold, You are there.

I had been angry at Him for taking her away and thought I could fix what He hadn't cared to. I had taken life and history into my own hands and lost. I had nothing left. I had no one and nothing left of me. I was strapped to a table about to be tortured and had no hope to save myself.

I desperately needed someone who was bigger than me, who was wiser than me, and was the only One who held time in His hand.

Your eyes saw my substance, being yet unformed.

And in Your book they all were written,

The days fashioned for me,

When as yet there were none of them.

I suddenly became conscious of the verse that had

been running through my head. It was Psalm 139. It was my grandma's favorite, and she had taught it to me when I was a little girl.

Slowly, thoughtfully, I finished the psalm.

Search me, O God, and know my heart;

Try me and know my anxieties;

And see if there is any wicked way in me,

And lead me in the way of everlasting.

Tears fell in sticky streams down my face.

Lord, I have nothing left to offer, nothing left to give. But all that is left of me is yours.

There was a strange sense of release. I couldn't call it peace, after all I was still strapped to the table with a mad scientist holding a syringe standing over me. But it felt like coming home. I didn't feel alone. Instead, I had a strange assurance that Someone bigger than me had a plan for my life.

The man smiled down at me. "You'll feel a prick."

He pushed the needle into the muscle of my upper arm.

I screamed through the duct tape.

I was still screaming when the mad scientist disappeared like vapor.

TRANSLATION KEY

HANNAH'S friend, Natalie, is British and tends to use British slang when nervous or upset. So if you feel like you might be "having kittens" one day, and would like to try Natalie's method of managing stress, here are a few phrases you will recognize from the book!

Bob's your uncle – phrase simply meaning, 'and that's that'

Daft cow – silly, or stupid, woman. Usually a term used affectionately with someone familiar

Donkey's years – if someone says they haven't seen you in 'donkey's years,' that means they haven't seen you in ages, or a very long time

Going to see a man about a dog – phrase used as an excuse when you were leaving but trying to hide your destination.

Loo – bathroom

Mad – crazy

Made Redundant – fired from a job

Snookered – If you are snookered, you are in trouble. In American English you might be up a creek without a paddle

Spanner in the Works- If someone throws a spinner in the works, he or she ruins a plan. In American English, an equivalent phrase is to "throw a wrench in it."

Tomorrow Timeline

G

F

Past events are listed in the letter key to the left.
This book's events are explained on the timeline itself.

While trying to escape from Katherine, Hannah makes a series of leaps through time. She jumps from the window and lands six months in the past, where she and Natalie try to escape only to have Hannah leap again to approx. 12 years in the past, where she finally leaps back to where she started the day.

K

J

I

E

C

1. Hannah and Seth travel back 1 year to save Abby.

2. Hannah and Seth save Abby, but Seth dies instead. Having just created a new timeline where Seth is dead, Hannah leaps forward 10 years.

Note:
Every time Hannah changes something in the past, the timeline is skewed and a new, altered future is created. The previous timeline ceases to exist.

B

A

Previous Events in the Yesterday series:

A - After traveling back 5 years, Hannah saves the Lawsons.
B - Hannah saves Wayne. Seth waits for her.
C - Hannah time travels with Seth into the past.
D - Hannah and Seth save Nicole Kraeger.
E - Hannah travels into the future.
F - Hannah meets Karis and tells her to send baby Hannah back in the time machine.
G - Karis and Jason send baby Hannah back in the time machine.
H - Baby Hannah arrives in the past and is adopted by the Kraegers.
I - Hannah saves Seth based on info from Karis's letter.
J – While on her honeymoon, Hannah travels back 1 year.
K – Abby dies. Hannah travels back 1 year.

'Yesterday' begins here.

H

D

Original Timeline

READER'S GUIDE

WHILE the *Yesterday* series is a fantastic story filled with twists and excitement, it is also intended as an extraordinary example of the way God works in our lives to accomplish His purpose and mold us into who He wants us to be.

Unfortunately, our journey through life usually isn't lined with roses. While God can see all of time, including our lives, laid out from beginning to end, we can only see a fraction. It's hard to understand how God can use horrible circumstances for His purpose and our good.

When faced with the overwhelming grief of losing her sister, Hannah doubts God's wisdom and faithfulness, and takes matters into her own hands. Hannah reacts as most of us would. If we possessed the power to change the past and avoid the grief, we would likely do it. We can't see the whole picture, but in our limited view, a tragedy seems like really poor planning on God's part. So why not fix it?

Tomorrow is the illustration of what would happen in our future when we are in charge, not God. Because of Hannah's anger and sin, a wedge is driven into her relationship with God. She tries to take control of her own life and make decisions according to her own wisdom. The results are disastrous. What follows is the story of Hannah's life falling apart to the point where she realizes God is the only one who can redeem any part of the mess she's created. She must yield control of her life to the One who owns it all, including the entirety of her past, present, and future.

As you read this book, did you relate to Hannah's desire to take control of her life? Could you relate to her anger at God and yet her need for him? Could you see any of your relationship with God in Hannah's?

My hope and prayer is that in reading the book and answering these questions, you will be able to see some of yourself in Hannah. I think it would be rare to encounter someone who hasn't felt anger toward God at some point and doubted His wisdom and providence. May Hannah's story encourage you through your own journey, and may you be drawn in close relationship to the One who knew all of your days before there was one of them.

Your eyes saw my substance, being yet unformed.
And in Your book they all were written,
The days fashioned for me,
When as yet there were none of them.
Psalm 139:16

Hannah admits that she has walked away from her faith, and now, without God and Seth, she is completely alone.

1. Have you ever felt completely alone? Either abandoned or isolated by your own choices?

Psalm 25:16-17

2. Even though Hannah has decided to forsake her relationship with God, is she really alone? Can you trace God's hand in Hannah's journey, even when she didn't welcome his influence?

Deuteronomy 31:6, Joshua 1:9, Psalm 91, Isaiah 41:10

3. What about your own life? Can you look back on a time when you felt alone, yet in retrospect see God's hand working?

Psalm 34:17-18, Psalm 139:7-12

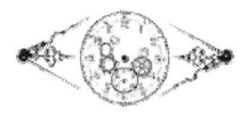

When faced with the reality of losing her husband and everyone she loved, Hannah is desperate to fix her life, and is determined to do it on her own. She says, "I couldn't trust anyone, especially God, to fix history the way I knew it needed to be.

4. Have you ever felt like God made a mistake? Maybe you couldn't understand why something happened, and you had a strong desire to fix it.

Proverbs 19:21

5. Have you ever been successful at fixing your problems on your own?

Colossians 1:21, Proverbs 16:9

Hannah had some pretty major consequences to trying to control her life and solve her problems without God.

6. What were some of the consequences for Hannah that directly resulted from her feelings toward God and her independent decisions?

7. What consequences have you see in your own life or the lives of others, when you try to go solo in solving your problems?

Lamentations 3:22-2, Romans 9:21

In this book, pretty much everything is stripped away from Hannah: her husband, family, friends, and reputation. Painted as a villain, despised by the public, and hunted by her enemy, she has no hope of a normal life. In despair, Hannah asks the question people have posed probably since the days of Adam: How could God let this happen?

8. What in your life has caused you to ask a similar question?

Matthew 10:29

9. As we look at the world, the realization is unavoidable: Bad things happen to good people. Life can be difficult, sprinkled with tragedy and trials that can't be understood this side of heaven. This is a very common question, one struggled

with by believers and unbelievers. What is your answer? Why do bad, unfair things happen in this world? Is there an easy answer?

John 16:33, Proverbs 16:4, Exodus 9:16

10. Having read the book, can you answer this question in terms of Hannah's life? Why did all of the difficult, bad things happen to Hannah? Was there a purpose behind the suffering?

1 Peter 1:6-9, Isaiah 45:6-7, Isaiah 55:8-11

Though Hannah has in some ways rejected her faith, she also cannot shake that longing to cry out to God. At one point, she says, "Even God seemed to be turning a blind eye to me, not that I had asked for anything different. Yet for the briefest of seconds, I longed to be able to call out to Him. But I had shut that door, and instead of standing at the door knocking, had the awful feeling that He had left me too."

11. Have you ever felt conflicted like Hannah? Can anger with God also be mixed with a longing for Him? Why is that?

Psalm 42

At the end of the book, when Hannah is at the lowest point she can possibly be, captured with no one to help, she remembers a scripture that she had memorized. The truth of Psalm 103 is what finally causes her to mend the gap in her relationship with God and surrender completely to Him.

12. Tell of a time when a verse of scripture ministered to you, made a difference in your actions, or came to bring meaning and blessing at just the right time.

Psalm 103:2, Corinthians 4:8-9

13. Do you have a favorite verse of scripture that ministers to you for where you are in your life right now?

Joshua 1:8, Psalm 119:11, Proverbs 22:17-18, 2 Timothy 3:16

At the end of her rope, Hannah finally surrenders, praying, "Lord, I have nothing left to offer, nothing left to give. But all that is left of me is yours."

14. Have you ever prayed a similar prayer to Hannah's?

Matthew 16:24-27, Proverbs 3:5-6, 1 John 2:1-6

If you used this guide in a group discussion, please pray with each other before closing in prayer.

NOTES:

_____

_____

_____

_____

_____

_____

_____

YESTERDAY SERIES

The Yesterday Series:

Book 1: Yesterday

Book 2: The Locket

Book 3: Today

Book 4: The Choice

Book 5: Tomorrow

Book 6: The Promise

FIND all the stories in the *Yesterday* series wherever fine books are sold.

MORE GREAT BOOKS

The Tru Exceptions Series:

Book 1: Baggage Claim

Book 2: Point of Origin

Book 3: Mirage

Stand-Alone Novels:

Secret Santa

The Romance of the Sugar Plum Fairy

Random Acts of Cupid

The Assumption of Guilt

SNEAK PEEK

ENJOY this special excerpt from *The Promise*, book 6 in the *Yesterday* series, available now wherever fine books are sold.

THE images in front of me shifted like changing TV channels. I saw trees and blue sky above me, and then there were tiles and fluorescent lights blinding my eyes. A few other channels flipped by in such rapid succession that I couldn't identify anything except blurs of color.

Then the swirling images stopped.

Everything around me came into focus.

I flexed my muscles, finding that I still couldn't move. I was strapped to the same table, and duct tape still sealed my mouth closed. But my surroundings were completely different.

Out of my peripheral vision, I saw something to my right that looked mechanical and vaguely familiar, but I couldn't see it well. A tall shelf was to my left.

I was still screaming, but through the duct tape, my screams sounded more like grunts. I heard footsteps, and suddenly, a man was standing over me. He had a full head of white hair and kind blue eyes that held a familiar sparkle.

He quickly unbuckled the straps. The tape stung horribly when he ripped it off my mouth. Rubbing the raw skin, I sat up.

"Please help me!" I cried. "He gave me something in an injection, and I don't know what it was!"

"It's okay," the man said calmly. "I can run some tests to figure out what they gave you. How are you feeling? Any pain?"

I opened my mouth to respond, but all coherent thought left my head as my vision collided with the mechanical thing that had been to my right.

It was massive, and I recognized it. I had seen it before. Actually, I had seen it twice before, and it was something I would never forget.

It was the catalyst that had both saved my life and sealed my fate.

It was a time machine.

"I was wondering when you would get here,

Hannah," the man said in his familiar teasing voice.

My breath caught. How did he know my name?

I looked at him, my brain denying what I automatically recognized in my heart as true. It couldn't be!

I slid off the table and turned a slow, full circle, my gaze finally resting on the tall shelving unit that had been on my left.

Perched on one of the middle shelves was a mini red remote control car. It was the same car I had once given a little boy for Christmas.

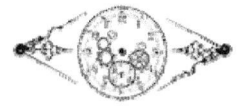

ABOUT THE AUTHOR

AMANDA TRU loves to write exciting books with plenty of unexpected twists. She figures she loses so much sleep writing the things, it's only fair she makes readers lose sleep with books they can't put down!

Amanda has always loved reading, and writing books has been a lifelong dream. A vivid imagination helps her write captivating stories in a wide variety of genres. Her current book list includes everything from holiday romances, to action-packed suspense, to a Christian time travel / romance series.

Amanda is a former elementary school teacher who now spends her days being mommy to three little boys and her nights furiously writing. Amanda and her family live in a small Idaho town where the number of cows outnumber the number of people.

Connect with Amanda Tru online:
http://amandatru.blogspot.com/

CONNECT ONLINE

Author site:
http://amandatru.blogspot.com/

Newsletter email sign up:
http://eepurl.com/ZQdw9

Facebook:
https://www.facebook.com/amandatru.author

Twitter:
https://twitter.com/TruAmanda

GooglePlus+:
https://plus.google.com/+AmandaTru

Pinterest:
http://www.pinterest.com/truamanda/

Goodreads:
https://www.goodreads.com/author/show/5374686.Amanda_Tru

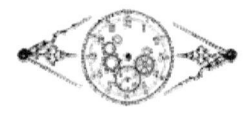